THE ANGEL TRAP

DARK WORLD: THE ANGEL TRIALS 3

MICHELLE MADOW

DREAMSCAPE PUBLISHING

NOAH

I SAT in the back seat of the Range Rover, Raven's head laid out on my lap as Sage sped north up the freeway. Sage drove fast. Way faster than any of the other cars on the road.

We needed to get to Chicago as quickly as possible. It didn't matter if a cop tried to stop us. If they did, we'd throw a pod of memory potion at them and make them forget they'd pulled us over in the first place.

Meanwhile, I ran my hands through Raven's hair, trying to will her to hold on. Her skin was red, charred, and blistered—because she'd held onto my heavenly knife and used it to slay a demon that *I* was supposed to kill.

Humans weren't supposed to handle heavenly weapons. While heavenly weapons felt normal to supernaturals, they burned hot to humans. Apparently it was like getting your hand near a hot stove.

It was a warning to them—letting them know to stay away from magic too powerful for them to handle.

Raven had been too stubborn to pay attention to the warning.

When Raven, Sage, and I were ambushed by a strong warrior demon and the strange red-eyed wolf shifter that accompanied him, Raven had gotten ahold of my heavenly dagger and killed the demon from behind.

Holding the heavenly weapon for so long had nearly killed her.

It still *was* killing her.

The injuries the heavenly weapon had inflicted on Raven were mortal, so healing potion hadn't worked on her. She'd been unconscious since killing the demon. Saving her should have been hopeless.

But she'd reached out to me through our imprint bond and let me know that vampire blood could cure her.

I'd never heard of vampire blood being able to do such a thing. Neither had Sage. But it was the last bit of hope I had to save Raven's life, so I'd grabbed onto it.

Unfortunately, if Raven was right and vampire blood could save her, the vampires had gone to a lot of trouble to keep this secret from all other supernaturals for centuries. Just *knowing* about the power of their blood could get us killed.

So we had three options.

One: Ask a vampire nearby in Nashville to borrow some of their blood and risk them likely sending their coven to kill us.

Two: Corner a nearby vampire in Nashville, kill them for their blood, give it to Raven, and hope no one ever found out.

Three: Go to a vampire we could trust and hope they'd be willing to save Raven.

I'd been seconds away from choosing option two—finding a random vampire and killing them for their blood. It wouldn't have been moral or right. But I wouldn't be able to live with myself if I let Raven die.

However, Sage had sworn there was a vampire she could trust in Chicago. A guy named Thomas Bettencourt.

I'd never heard of him before. Then again, I didn't know much about the supernatural community outside of my hometown of the Vale. Everything else I knew had been what Sage had told me during the past few weeks when we'd been working together to kill demons.

She'd certainly never mentioned a vampire in Chicago by the name of Thomas Bettencourt.

But I trusted Sage. So if she said we could trust this

Thomas guy, I believed her. Plus, Raven had sent a burst of positive energy in my direction when Sage had mentioned Thomas.

Raven didn't want me killing a random vampire to save her life, either. Not when there was another option on the table.

Which was why we were now driving as fast as possible from Nashville to Chicago. The map on Sage's phone said we could get there in seven and a half hours, but with the way she was speeding, we'd get there sooner than that.

I studied Raven's face, finding her beautiful despite her red, charred skin.

Was it just me, or was the red a deeper color than before?

She was getting worse.

If I couldn't hear her weak heartbeat and feel her warm energy through our imprint bond, I would have thought she was already dead.

What if we didn't make it in time? What if she took her final breath right here in this car, before we had a chance to save her?

My heart descended into darkness at the thought. I'd had so many awful things happen to me in the past few months—I couldn't handle Raven dying on top of all of it.

Not before I told her about our imprint bond.

If she died, surely it was some sort of cosmic punishment for what I'd done at the Vale.

But I couldn't let my mind go down that path. If I did —if I let myself think about all the terrible things I'd done and witnessed—I'd get pulled further and further down a spiral of defeat.

I needed to distract myself.

What better way to do that than to learn more about this mysterious vampire that Sage trusted with her life?

"So." I focused on Sage as she expertly weaved her way around two cars blocking our way. "I think it's time you tell me about Thomas Bettencourt."

2

NOAH

SAGE'S EYES hardened the moment I said Thomas's name.

I recognized that look. It was heartbreak.

Whoever this vampire was, he'd done a serious number on her.

"Thomas is the leader of the Bettencourt coven," she said, keeping all emotion out of her voice. "They're a powerful coven in Chicago, and they all live in the Bettencourt Hotel. They get their blood from the humans who stay there as guests."

"They must be able to afford a lot of memory potion," I guessed.

That was the only way a vampire coven could stay in one place for so long—if they could afford enough memory potion to keep their victims unaware of the fact that they were being fed on. All supernaturals hid from humans. Our community had gotten especially strict about it in the past century, as humans had grown in number and developed weapons that were extremely dangerous—even to us.

Yes, we were strong enough to overpower humans like they were insects. But against a nuclear bomb?

That wasn't something we wanted to test out.

The vampires were especially strict about keeping themselves hidden. Most vampires lived in one of the six kingdoms—one on each continent—but there were a handful of covens and rogue vampires spread about as well. If a coven or rogue vampire got too reckless and the humans nearby got suspicious, the closest vampire kingdom swooped in real fast to put an end to it.

If the caught vampires were drinking from their victims but allowing them to live, they were usually allowed to take up residence in one of the kingdoms.

If they were draining the humans dry, they were killed.

The only vampire kingdom that allowed their vampires to kill was the Tower. But the Tower was in South America, so their laws didn't apply in the United States.

Vampires caught out of line in the United States were handled by the Vale.

"They can certainly afford it," Sage said. "But I'm not sure how often they have to use it."

"Really." I leaned forward, intrigued, keeping Raven's head steady on my lap the entire time. "Why's that?"

"Because Thomas isn't just any regular vampire," Sage said. "He's a vampire prince."

I whistled, not bothering to hide that I was impressed. Vampire royalty were far stronger than their common counterparts. Because in addition to their regular supernatural powers, they could use compulsion.

Which meant they could look someone in the eye and command them to do whatever they said.

When it came to erasing memories, memory potion was always a better bet over compulsion. But compulsion could definitely be used to make a human forget about an encounter or two with a vampire.

It explained how Thomas and his coven had been able to live in one place undetected for so long.

"What's His Highness doing here?" I asked, not bothering to hide the sarcasm from my tone. "Shouldn't he be in his kingdom, doing whatever it is that princes do?"

"He was turned by Mary of the Haven," Sage said. "In the 1930s—after the Great War—Mary searched for strong humans she thought could become powerful vampires and turned them, so she could keep the Haven as protected as possible."

I nodded, not surprised at all. The Great War of the 1920s was one of the darkest times in supernatural history. It made sense that Mary, the ruler of the Haven, had wanted to increase her numbers to keep the Haven protected.

As the most peaceful kingdom in the world, the vampires of the Haven drank only animal blood. But this made them weaker than vampires that fed on human blood. So they needed other ways to protect themselves. Before the Great War, the vampires of the Haven were already well protected thanks to their alliance with the local tiger shifters. But increasing their population with more powerful vampires—vampires with unique abilities, like Rosella who could see the future—made them even stronger. Everyone knew not to mess with the Haven.

"Thomas was our age in the 1930s—during the Great Depression," Sage continued. "He had a talent for machines—tinkering with them and getting them to work—but he was only making pennies. Those were hard times back then. So when Mary came to him and asked if he wanted to be turned into a vampire, he took her up on the offer."

"Hold up," I said. "Mary made him an *offer?*"

I didn't think vampires gave humans an option on if they wanted to turn or not. The vampires I knew—which honestly, weren't many—had been turned against their wills.

"The Haven is a kingdom dedicated to peace," Sage said. "Any vampire willing to survive on animal blood is welcome there. And when a vampire of the Haven turns a human, that human is always given a choice. Thomas saw turning as the best chance out of poverty, so he took it. He had access to money in the Haven, and he wanted to wire the money to his family to keep them comfortable for the rest of their lives."

"But now he lives in Chicago," I said, and Sage nodded. "If he was turned by Mary, shouldn't he still be in the Haven?"

"Mary doesn't want any resident of the Haven to be a prisoner there," she said. "All Haven residents are free to leave, although it's their responsibility to remain under the radar wherever they go. Mary isn't responsible for anything they do if they leave the Haven. Thomas *did* live there for the first decade after he was turned, but the Haven is more of a… traditional place. They're not up to date on the latest technology. As Thomas saw glimpses of the progress the outside world was taking, he yearned to be a part of it. So he left, bought the hotel in Chicago, and turned it into the Bettencourt of today."

"It sounds like a fancy place." I stroked Raven's hair as I spoke. Even though she was unconscious, I needed to remind her I was there for her and that I wasn't going anywhere—not until she was healed, and not *ever*.

"You have no idea," Sage said. "Thomas turned the hotel into a fortress."

"I can't wait to see it," I said, since I *was* curious. "But when I asked about Thomas, I wasn't asking about his personal history."

Sage stared straight ahead, saying nothing.

"I was asking about your relationship with him." Apparently she needed me to spell it out for her.

"I know you were," she said. "And I was purposefully avoiding talking about it."

"Why?" I asked.

"Because Thomas and I have a... complicated history." She tightened her grip around the steering wheel, the broken look in her eyes returned.

"How complicated?" I was more curious than ever. Sage was a straight shooter, so whatever had happened between her and Thomas must have been pretty bad.

"*Beyond* complicated." She took a deep breath, and then let it out all at once. "Because once upon a time, Thomas Bettencourt and I were engaged."

3

NOAH

"What?" I didn't know what I'd expected, but it certainly hadn't been that. "You mean engaged to be *married*?"

She glanced back at me in the rearview mirror and raised an eyebrow. "What other type of 'engaged' is there?" she asked.

"I don't know," I said. "I just didn't know you were ever engaged."

"That's because I never told you," she said. "It's not something I ever talk about. But you're going to find out at some point while we're there, so..." She shrugged, letting the statement hang in the air.

"What happened?" I asked, since obviously something had happened. If it hadn't, then Sage would be married right now.

That was *so* weird to think about.

"He broke off the engagement and hasn't spoken to me since." She shrugged again, but I could tell from the pain shining in her eyes that it was hard for her to talk about.

"What a dick," I said the only appropriate response I could think of in that moment.

"Tell me about it." She rolled her eyes and chuckled. "I was only eighteen. I didn't handle it well."

"I don't think that's something anyone can 'handle well,'" I said. "It just straight out sucks."

"It *did* straight out suck." She smiled—this time for real. "But when I say I didn't handle it well, I mean that right afterward, I kissed every shifter in California trying to find someone to imprint with. I thought if I imprinted, it would get rid of the hole in my heart that Thomas had created by breaking our engagement."

"And you didn't imprint on any one of those guys?" I asked.

"Oh, I didn't limit myself to guys," she said mischievously. "But correct. Out of *all* the shifters I kissed—and trust me, there were a lot of them—I didn't imprint on one of them. Not *one*. I've never imprinted on anyone. I'm honestly starting to wonder if I'm defective or something."

"If you're defective, then I guess I am, too," I said. "I

mean, who's ever heard of a shifter imprinting on a human?"

"Good point," she said. "Two defective shifters. I suppose that explains why we're such good friends."

"Yeah." I was silent for a few seconds, reflecting on what she'd just told me. "But there's one important thing I don't get," I eventually said.

"What?" she asked.

"If Thomas Bettencourt broke off your engagement and hasn't spoken to you since, why do you trust him with Raven's life?" I asked. "With *all* our lives?" I needed to add that last part, since we had every reason to believe that vampires would kill us if they knew we knew about the healing properties their blood had on humans.

"Because despite what he did, Thomas loved me," she said sadly. "He shattered my heart, but he'd never kill me —or anyone I cared about. Especially since the Bettencourt coven is allied with the Montgomery pack. Plus, I know Thomas. He's practical, logical, and he'll agree to any deal as long as it benefits him. And he's *very* skilled at figuring out ways for things to benefit him. It'll be fine."

"Good," I said. "Because I don't care what Thomas wants. I'll do anything to save Raven's life."

I studied Raven's burnt features, guilt tearing through my heart once more at the sight of her.

She was like this because of me. Because I'd failed at protecting her.

If we didn't get to Chicago in time...

I shook my head, refusing to think about it. Raven was strong. Stubborn. Even though she wasn't conscious, I knew she was in there, and that she knew we were on the way to get her help. She was going to hold on. Not just for me, but for her mom. After all, that was why we were here in the first place. Raven needed to get to Avalon to go through the Angel Trials to turn into a Nephilim so she could gain the strength she needed to save her mom, who'd been abducted by the greater demon Azazel.

She had too much left to do to give up now. Everything we were going through was building her strength so she'd survive the Angel Trials. When Raven and I had gone to see Rosella at the Santa Monica Pier, Rosella had said that Raven needed the experiences she'd have with me on my hunt to survive the Trials. The vampire seer had *insisted* that Raven accompany me.

At first, I'd thought that was ridiculous. I hadn't thought a human could help Sage and me. I thought she'd be useless. Worse than useless—I'd thought she'd be a burden.

But I was wrong. Raven *had* helped us.

Because as much as it wounded my pride to think it, I wasn't sure I would have beaten that warrior demon in the alley without her help.

And once she was healed, I'd make sure she never felt unappreciated ever again.

4

SAGE

Noah was too worried about Raven to get any sleep on the drive to Chicago. Understandably so. I didn't bother asking if he wanted me to take a turn driving, because there was no chance he was leaving Raven's side in the backseat.

It was a good thing I'd taken a nap yesterday afternoon before we left to hunt the demon in Nashville. Noah always said that one of the most important parts of demon hunting was to make sure you slept whenever there was time to do so, since we never knew when we'd be able to sleep next.

I was too anxious about seeing Thomas again to sleep, anyway. Not because I didn't think he'd help Raven—I meant what I'd told Noah earlier about trusting him with my life.

But because it was going to be so awkward to face him again after he'd humiliated me by breaking our engagement. At the time, he'd given me some crappy excuse about realizing it was silly to think a marriage between a vampire and a shifter could work out.

I didn't buy it. I might have been young when we fell in love, but the love between us had been real. He should have told me the truth about why he'd called off the wedding.

Which was why I hadn't spoken to him since.

Noah and I remained quiet for the rest of the drive, lost in our own thoughts. Finally, soon after sunrise, we entered the Chicago city limits.

After getting off the freeway, I didn't need the GPS to tell me where to go anymore.

I knew how to get to the Bettencourt just as well as I knew how to get home. And the closer we got to the hotel, the more my stomach flip-flopped like crazy.

I wanted to turn around and drive as far away as possible. But of course I didn't do that.

Raven's life was more important than my wounded pride.

It didn't take long until we were there. With its carved stone facade, the Bettencourt screamed elegance the moment we turned onto the Magnificent Mile and saw its shiny gold overhang taking up the majority of the block. Even though I'd been there many times before, I never ceased to be awed by the hotel's sleek elegance.

The building was imposing and impressive—just like Thomas.

But I didn't stop at the front of the hotel. Instead, I headed around to the garage and drove down the ramp toward the gate.

It didn't open when I pulled up.

"This garage is for residents of the Bettencourt only," an automated voice said from the speaker next to the gate. "If you're a guest at the hotel, please pull around to the front entrance, and our valet will be happy to park your car for you."

"I need a private audience with Thomas Betten- court," I spoke into the machine, knowing *someone* would hear me. "Now. And I need to park myself. In his private lot."

I glanced around at the ceilings and walls. While invisible to the naked eye, there were more cameras in the Bettencourt than there were in a casino in a Vegas hotel. I had no doubt that someone was watching us at this very moment.

And that person was likely Thomas.

A few seconds passed with no response. I drummed my fingers on the steering wheel, getting out nervous energy as I waited. Noah continued to stroke Raven's hair, his eyes growing more panicked by the second.

Once five minutes passed, I worried that my plan to drop by without warning had been really stupid. But this wasn't something I could spring on Thomas through a phone call.

He needed to hear what we had to say in person.

Finally, the intercom clicked. Someone had picked up.

I stared at it, my throat tightening so much that I wasn't sure I'd be able to speak. What if it was Thomas?

I never imagined that the first time I'd speak to him since he'd dumped me would be through the intercom system in the parking garage at his hotel.

"Ms. Montgomery," a female voice said, and I relaxed—slightly. "You have permission to enter Mr. Bettencourt's private garage. Will you be needing directions?"

"No." I was so nervous that I had to force the word out.

I hated that I still cared so much.

"Very well," she said. "Please proceed. Mr. Bettencourt is waiting for you in his penthouse."

The gate opened, and I took the few turns that led to Thomas's private garage. Eventually, I pulled up to a dead end—a narrow passageway that faced a concrete wall—and put the car into park.

"Is this Thomas's private garage?" Noah glanced around, looking confused.

"No." I stared straight ahead.

"Then why'd you stop?"

I couldn't blame him for being confused. It likely looked like I'd stopped because I was nervous about seeing Thomas and wasn't sure I could continue.

While the first part was true—the part about being nervous to see Thomas—the second part wasn't.

"Just wait," I said. "You'll see."

The floor rumbled beneath us, and it clicked, like it was coming loose. Then we started to slowly lower down into the ground through a car-sized opening.

Half a minute later, we stared around at a titanium-enclosed space lined with dozens of cars. They ranged from antique models that looked like they'd come straight out of the early twentieth century, to futuristic-looking sports cars, with a few funky ones thrown in for good measure.

My favorite had always been the DeLorean, mainly because it was equipped with its own flux capacitor. Not a working one, of course—time travel didn't exist. But it was designed to flux and everything.

I'd always remember the time Thomas had let me drive it out of the city and take it up to eighty-eight miles per hour. That day had been incredible.

But I shook the memory out of my head, not wanting to dwell on the past. It would only get me upset.

Despite the thought of seeing Thomas again driving me crazy on the inside, I was determined to appear as cool and collected as possible. Which meant staying focused on our mission—saving Raven's life.

Refocusing, I drove off the moving platform and glanced into the rearview mirror, watching it rise up again behind us.

"*This* is Thomas's personal garage," I told Noah, driving around the underground car fortress to search for an empty spot.

"These cars aren't all his." Noah gazed around at them in awe. "Are they?"

"They are," I said. "But he lets members of his coven take them out. Well, certain cars. His favorites are only to be touched by him."

I stopped once I found an empty spot next to the elevator. I knew this spot—it was always reserved for one of Thomas's favorite cars. He must have had it cleared for us sometime between when we'd arrived and now.

He must have seen through the cameras that there was an unconscious girl in the back of the car.

Clearing the spot for us had been thoughtful, and I

hated that. Well, I was grateful, since it would be better for Noah not to have to carry Raven as far. But I hated that it made me remember how considerate Thomas could be.

We got out of the car, Noah carrying Raven protectively in his arms. Her skin looked redder than when we'd left Nashville, and I could barely hear the pounding of her heart. She was holding on, but barely. It was a good thing we'd arrived when we did.

The moment we approached the glass doors that led to the elevator, a red light on the side of them turned green. They parted to let us in.

I gave a slight nod of thanks, knowing that a camera somewhere would see it.

The up button on the elevator was already pressed, and it opened for us a second later. The elevator was just like I remembered—polished marble floors and mirrored walls with simple patterns along the edges. It gave the illusion of the interior going on for miles.

I faced the front, not wanting to look at my reflection. The last thing I'd done before Raven's injury was fight a red-eyed wolf shifter. I'd healed quickly, and since I'd fought the shifter in wolf form, my clothes were intact and there was no blood on me. But my hair was a wreck, my makeup was a mess, and I had huge circles under my eyes from driving all night.

This *really* wasn't how I wanted to look when I saw Thomas again for the first time.

But I had no choice. Because once the doors shut, the elevator shot up to the penthouse without anyone needing to press a button.

5

SAGE

ONCE WE REACHED the top floor, the doors opened straight into Thomas's foyer. We stepped into the bright, modern penthouse, where Thomas was waiting in the living room.

As always, he wore a tailored suit fitted perfectly for him. He stared at me with those dark, soulful eyes, and suddenly I felt like a teen again, left speechless at the sight of him. It was like no time had passed since the last time we'd seen each other. It didn't help that he looked exactly the same, since vampires were immortal and all.

My cheeks flushed with the knowledge that due to his heightened senses, he could likely hear how quickly my heart was pounding. I stepped out of the elevator, trying to look anywhere but straight into his eyes.

Unfortunately, my body betrayed me. It was impossible to look away from him for long.

Noah rushed past me, hurried to one of the couches, and laid Raven down upon it.

For the first time since we'd entered, Thomas broke his gaze away from mine to look at Raven. His eyes widened when he saw her. Almost like he recognized her?

But that was impossible. He was more likely appalled that Noah had just placed a dirty, nearly dead human girl on his pristine white sofa.

"Sage Montgomery," Thomas finally spoke, my name flowing from his lips like music. He was poised as always, and I wished I had just an *ounce* of his composure right now. "I assume there's an important reason why you and your shifter friend here stopped by with no warning, looking like you've just driven all night, to drop a dying human onto my sofa?"

I swallowed and clenched my fists, needing to get my wits back so I could do what we'd come here to do and save Raven's life.

I'd practiced this in my mind during the long drive here. I could do this.

"Her name is Raven." I glanced at where Raven was motionless on the sofa. Noah sat beside her, cradling her head in his lap. The desperation in his eyes gave me the strength to continue. "How I got to be traveling with her and Noah is a long story, and one I'll tell later. The important part for now is that she and Noah have imprinted on each other. She's received mortal injuries that can't be treated with healing potion. She needs your blood to save her life."

Thomas stared at me and placed a hand in his pants pocket. A nervous habit of his.

I wasn't sure what he'd expected me to say, but it certainly hadn't been that.

He raised an eyebrow, challenging me. "Why does she need my blood?" he asked.

"Because vampire blood has the power to heal humans." I squared my shoulders and leveled my gaze with his, not wanting to give him a reason to contradict me. If I looked unsure, he'd know I wasn't sure if I believed it myself. "Even from mortal injuries."

"How did you come to know this?" he asked.

"I'm not the one who knew." I glanced over at Raven. "Raven did. She communicated with Noah through their imprint bond to let him know it was the only way to save her."

"And you came knocking on my door because I'm the only vampire you didn't think would kill you for being privy to this top secret information." He studied me suspiciously, making me wonder if I was mistaken in thinking he still valued my life.

"Was I wrong?" I maintained a strong appearance, stopping myself from looking around the penthouse to search for an escape.

Now that we were up here, there *was* no escape. Thomas controlled every bit of technology in this building. If he wanted us dead, we wouldn't stand a chance of getting out alive.

"If I wanted to kill you, you'd be dead already," he confirmed.

I let out a breath, relieved and slightly terrified at the same time. I wasn't used to him treating me like this—the same way he treated everyone else. I'd always been special to him. When we'd been together, Thomas had been protective, open, and loving.

To the rest of the world, he was as cold as the machines he controlled.

That was the side of him I was seeing now. It was like he'd never loved me at all. Like I was a stranger to him.

My heart felt like it was breaking all over again—just like it had on the day he'd called off our engagement.

But like he'd said, if I were truly a stranger to him, I'd be dead right now.

So I refused to let his emotional walls set me off course.

"Raven doesn't have long. She needs your blood to live." I hated begging—especially in the current circumstances—but I'd do it to save Raven. As crazy as it was, Raven had quickly turned into one of the closest friends I'd ever had. I couldn't just let her die. "Please."

Thomas stepped closer to Raven, examining her. His expression didn't change in the slightest. "She's a human, yet imprinted on a shifter." He zeroed in on Noah, looking down at him suspiciously. "How's that possible?"

"I don't know." Noah stared up at Thomas and held Raven's limp body protectively, as if warning Thomas not to hurt her. "But as far as I know, it's the first time a shifter has ever imprinted on someone outside of our species. Who knows if it'll ever happen again? It might not. So if we want to understand what allowed her to imprint on me, then you have to save her. Now."

I tensed, prepared for Thomas to react poorly to being ordered to do anything.

But instead of getting angry, he smirked. "Point received." He nodded. "I'll save your human companion."

Noah and I thanked him at the same time, but Thomas held a hand up to cut us off.

I pressed my lips together, waiting for what he was going to say next. I'd *hoped* he'd save Raven because a part of him still loved me and wanted to make me happy, but I'd prepared myself for that not being the case.

It was enough that we'd gotten this far without him killing us. It would have been foolish to truly believe that the man who'd broken our engagement over a *phone call* would save a friend of mine's life simply to make me happy.

"I'll save your companion," Thomas repeated. "But only on a few conditions."

6

SAGE

"Of course," I said, not surprised at all. "What are your conditions?"

"Before I get into that, you should know how vampire blood will affect your human companion." Thomas sat down on one of the armchairs and motioned for me to do the same on the one next to him.

I did as he wanted, sitting on the edge of the seat as I waited for him to continue.

"My blood will heal her, as you already know," he said. "But it will also give her vampire abilities for twenty-four hours."

"Seriously?" I widened my eyes, not having expected that. "So humans can drink vampire blood every day and have vampire abilities without having to actually *be* vampires?"

"Technically, yes," he said. "Which is another reason why we keep the effects of our blood secret. The last thing we need to deal with is crazed humans hunting us down for our blood."

"Makes sense," I said.

"But while our blood will give humans our abilities, it causes a lot of stress on their bodies," he continued. "A human who constantly drinks vampire blood will age much faster than they would naturally."

"How fast?" I asked.

"A few experiments have been done in the past." He waved his hand, as if the idea of experimenting on humans wasn't disturbing to him in the slightest. "In secret, of course. It's not an exact science. If a strong, healthy human drinks vampire blood for a year straight, they'll age about five human years. But it could age them as much as ten years. It depends on the individual."

I did some quick math in my head. While it would lower the human lifespan significantly, I had no doubts that there were plenty of humans who would take ten to twenty years of supernatural abilities over a full life as a human.

I also couldn't help realizing that a few weeks of drinking vampire blood wouldn't age a human significantly. Meaning that if Raven drank vampire blood for the remainder of our hunt, she'd be a lot stronger and able to help.

But I'd propose that idea later. Right now, we didn't know how much longer she had left. I needed to finalize this agreement with Thomas and save her life.

"I see the wheels in your mind spinning," Thomas said with a knowing smile.

I dug my fingernails into my palms, hating how he knew me so well. It was yet another reminder of what we'd had and lost.

Despite my natural instinct to return his smile, I forced myself to keep a straight face. "Raven doesn't have a lot of time," I said what I was thinking. "What are your conditions?"

"I'm getting to that." He held a finger up for me to be patient. "Like I was saying, your human companion—Raven—will have vampire abilities for twenty-four hours after drinking vampire blood. We can't have anyone seeing her and thinking she's a vampire, and then being confused when she returns to being human. It'll ruin the secret of our blood. So she'll need to remain hidden in a secure room in the penthouse until the supernatural abilities wear off."

There went my plan of having Raven drink vampire blood for the remainder of the demon hunt. If Thomas wouldn't let anyone see Raven while she was under the influence of his blood, he'd never let her go out and hunt with us.

Oh well. It was a good plan while it had lasted.

But we'd gotten this far with her having no supernatural abilities, and we only had one more demon left to slay until we had all ten teeth to present to the Earth Angel at Avalon. We could keep her safe until then.

"That's fine," I agreed.

"Great." Noah looked down at Raven anxiously before returning his gaze to Thomas. "So are you ready to do this or what?"

"That was only the first of my conditions." Thomas chuckled. "I have three more."

"Let's hear them." Noah narrowed his eyes at Thomas, like he was challenging him to see just how far he'd go to save Raven's life.

Hopefully Thomas didn't want anything *too* extreme.

But knowing him, I doubted it.

"Firstly, both of you must make a blood oath with me that you'll tell no one about what you know about vampire blood," he said. "Once Raven is healed, she won't be allowed to leave the penthouse until she makes the blood oath too."

"Got it." I nodded in agreement, and Noah did the same.

Blood oaths were the strongest promises supernaturals could make. Even humans could enter into blood oaths, as long as it was with a supernatural. If someone tried to go against a blood oath they'd made, their blood would turn against them and kill them. It was thought to be one of the most painful deaths imaginable.

I avoided entering into blood oaths—most supernaturals did. I'd never entered into one before. I'd offered one to Leia, the alpha of the rougarou pack in New Orleans, to ensure our safety. Luckily, I hadn't needed to go through with it since we'd gained trust in each other and made an alliance instead.

This blood oath would be my first. But it was one I was willing to make.

"And your second condition?" Noah tapped his foot on the floor, getting antsier by the second. I couldn't blame him, since Raven's life was on the line and Thomas was acting like we had all the time in the world.

"I'll require a private audience with Raven immediately after she's healed," he said.

"Is that to get her to make the blood oath?" Noah asked. "Because she'll be a lot more comfortable making it if she has people she trusts by her side." His fingers were now intertwined with Raven's, his hand gripping her limp one. The blisters on her skin were popping and cracking, revealing more burned skin underneath.

I couldn't imagine how much pain she was in. No

wonder her body had shut down and forced her into this comatose state.

"It's not about the blood oath—you're free to be in the room with her during that," Thomas said. "I want a private audience with her, and no, I'm not going to tell you why. You either agree to the condition or you don't. If you don't, you know where the exit is." He glanced toward the elevator in the foyer.

"You won't hurt her?" Noah asked. "Or lay a finger on her?"

Thomas glanced back and forth between Noah and Raven, as if understanding Noah's concern. "I'll be having a discussion with her," he said. "That's all."

"All right," Noah agreed. "But if I hear you tried anything with her…" He glared at Thomas, the threat lingering in the air.

"I urge you not to forget that I'm helping you here," Thomas reminded him. "I'm the only one who *can* help you right now. Threaten me again and we're done."

The two of them were so different—like fire and ice. But right now, Thomas had the power, so Noah backed down.

"Understood," Noah said.

"I'm a man of my word," Thomas replied. "I have no interest in harming your girlfriend. I only want to have a chat with her—privately."

It took everything I had to resist rolling my eyes when he called himself a man of his word. Because as far as I was aware, men of their word didn't make marriage proposals and then take them back with an obviously fake explanation why.

But as easy as it would have been to say something snarky in reply, I held my tongue. I wasn't about to risk him retracting his offer to save Raven's life because I was still bitter about the way he'd broken my heart.

"I see no problems with that," I said instead, looking to Noah to keep myself cool. "What about you?"

Noah watched me closely, and while I could see he was still worried, he relaxed significantly knowing that I was okay with Thomas's proposition. "I agree to the term." His voice was stiff, and he turned back to face Thomas. "But you said you had three more conditions. What's the third?"

"My final condition is the most important one." Thomas's dark eyes stared straight at me, as if he was seeing into my soul. "Because while it will be interesting to save Raven to try to understand how she—a human—imprinted on a shifter, it's not why I'm entering into this deal."

"Then why are you doing it?" I asked.

"Because I see this is important to you, and I care

about you," he said. "You *know* I care about you—you wouldn't have come to me for help otherwise."

"I know you don't want me dead." Every muscle in my body immediately went on guard—especially my heart. "There's a difference."

"Not really." He leaned back in his chair, looking smugly confident in his assumption. "The knowledge you have about vampire blood has been kept within our species for as long as we've existed. The only people I wouldn't kill for knowing about it are the ones I care about. Those people are few and far between. As for everyone else… this secret is more important than their lives."

I nodded, since this was why we'd come to Thomas instead of any other vampire.

He cared about me—like someone cared for a pet they'd grown fond of. But he'd never truly wanted to marry me.

He loved the challenge of getting me to say yes to marrying him more than actually wanting to be with me.

I'd hoped that someday I'd be able to move on and get over it. But seeing him now re-opened the wound I didn't think would ever truly heal.

"Where are you going with this?" I wished he would

get to the point so we could agree to his deal, heal Raven, and get out of here.

"I hurt you deeply all those years ago when I realized it wasn't in your best interest to spend your life with me, and I'm sorry about the pain I caused you." He focused on me like I was the only person in the room, and I could barely breathe as I waited for where he was going with this. "So my final condition is that you grant me your forgiveness."

7

SAGE

I BLINKED A FEW TIMES, unsure I heard that right.

Had Thomas just *required* that I forgive him for breaking our engagement and leaving my heart in pieces?

From the way he sat perfectly straight, awaiting my response, it was clear that yes—he was being completely serious.

And from the way Noah watched me with fire in his eyes, clutching onto Raven like a reminder about what was at stake, it was clear he wanted me to agree.

This was messed up on so many levels.

If I didn't know Thomas, I would have felt pressured to say yes—for Raven's sake. But I *did* know Thomas. And I knew that when he made deals, his terms were always up for negotiation.

So you could bet I was going to negotiate the hell out of this one.

"You can't just *demand* my forgiveness," I balked, sounding as repulsed by the proposition as I felt. "Emotions can't be that easily controlled, and they certainly can't be bargained for."

Thomas's eyes flashed with something—either disappointment or pain—but he hid it too quickly to give me any time to read into it. "Anything can be bargained for," he said simply.

"Not that." I didn't miss a beat. "I agree to your first two terms, but not the last."

"Sage," Noah warned, looking like he was about to spring up and force me to agree.

Thomas held a hand up to stop Noah, his eyes locked on mine. "I respect your stance," he said, calm as always. "So I won't ask for your forgiveness. At least not yet. Instead, I ask that immediately following my private audience with Raven, you allow me to take you on a date."

"What?" This shocked me more than his demand for my forgiveness. "*You* were the one who dumped *me*. Why do you want to take me on a date?"

"Because you're correct that it's presumptuous of me to bargain for your forgiveness," he said. "But your forgiveness is still something I desire. By taking you out on a date, I'll have a chance to earn it."

I pressed my lips together, not wanting to say yes. It was hard enough for me to come here at all—to see Thomas and be reminded of everything I'd lost.

A date with him was something else entirely. He wasn't one to do anything halfway, and that included dates. I knew better than to expect this date to be something as simple as dinner and a movie. Whatever he had in mind was going to be over the top extraordinary—a romantic whirlwind designed to impress, amaze, and most importantly, to seduce.

If I agreed to a date, I'd be giving him the power to break my heart all over again.

I'd come so far since our break up. It had been hard to sweep up the shattered pieces of my heart, but I'd managed. I'd gone from a never-ending pit of feeling bleak, lonely, and depressed to becoming confident, strong, and secure.

I refused to go back to where I'd been after he'd dumped me. I wouldn't give him that kind of power over me ever again.

But then I glanced at Raven—well, at what was left of her. She'd been so strong and brave to come with Noah and me on our hunt, despite only just learning about the supernatural world. Then she'd suffered through immeasurable pain by holding onto the heavenly knife to help us against the warrior demon and his red-eyed shifter pet.

If she could bear the pain of holding onto a heavenly weapon that burned her to the core, surely I could bear one date with the man who'd broken my heart.

I needed to pull it together. Not just for Raven, but also for Noah. I could do this—for them.

"All right." I tried to sound as cool and unattached as Thomas as I accepted his offer. "You have yourself a deal."

8

RAVEN

I AWOKE WITH A JOLT, sucking in a deep breath that burned as it made its way through my lungs.

I'd once heard that the most painful breath you'd ever take was as a newborn, when you filled your lungs with air for the first time. That was apparently why all babies cried after being born.

I couldn't imagine that being worse than this.

Luckily the pain subsided a moment later, and I stared up into the eyes of Noah, Sage, and a man a few years older than me who I didn't recognize. And while I felt like me... I also didn't.

My vision was crisper than ever. I could see ridges and patterns in Noah's brown eyes that I hadn't seen before. With my intake of breath came an influx of smells, too. Warm, woodsy smells from both Noah and Sage, and a sharp, metallic smell from the man I didn't know. There was also a trio of dull beating sounds somewhere in the background.

Was I hearing their hearts?

I blinked for a few moments, trying to center myself. I'd gone under anesthesia once—when I was eighteen and had my wisdom teeth removed—and the fuzziness I'd felt upon waking up then was similar to what I was feeling now.

So I thought back to the last thing I remembered— the fight with the demon and the red-eyed shifter in the alley in Nashville. Noah and Sage had been struggling with the fight. I'd used the heavenly knife to slay the demon myself.

Judging by the fact that I was here and not dead, I guessed I'd succeeded in slaying the demon. But why were my senses so heightened? Was it because I'd held onto the heavenly knife for so long?

"What happened?" I pressed my fingers to my fore-head, sounding just as groggy as I felt. I vaguely remembered having intense, detailed dreams while I'd been asleep, but they'd nearly faded away completely. Now I was lying on a couch in a sleek, modern room that was *definitely* not the hotel room we'd had in Nashville. "Where are we?"

"It worked." Noah grinned, and the next thing I knew, he leaned down and kissed me.

His touch sent warm tingles flowing through my body, and as I kissed him back, I heard his heart and mine start beating in time with each other. I also felt something else—relief.

But that feeling wasn't mine. It was Noah's.

The connection between us was stronger than ever—just like when he'd kissed me the first time in that bar in New Orleans.

He eventually broke away, caressing my face as if I was a precious jewel and he never wanted to let go. "Don't scare me like that ever again," he said.

"Scare you?" I sat up, thinking back again to what had happened in the alley. "From what I remember, I *saved* you."

"By using a weapon that's deadly for humans to hold and nearly getting yourself killed," he said. "You *would* have died, if we hadn't used vampire blood to save you."

"What?" I touched my head again, trying to make sense of it all. I couldn't even think about Noah's kissing me and what it meant between the two of us. I'd definitely think about it later, but not now. Because the insanely crisp vision, the intensely strong smells, being able to hear heartbeats... those senses were beyond anything I'd ever experienced.

They were *supernatural*. And if I was feeling like this because of vampire blood…

"What did you do to save me?" Suspicion gnawed at me, and I swallowed, bracing myself for what was to come. "Did you turn me into a vampire?"

"No," said the man I didn't know, and all of us immediately looked to him. He wore a perfectly pressed suit, and with his classic haircut and clean-shaven face, he radiated the aura of a high-powered businessman. "If I'd turned you into a vampire, you'd be out of your mind with the need to drain a human of their blood right now."

"You're a vampire?" I asked him, since I knew only vampires could turn humans into one of their kind. I'd learned that during the "supernatural lessons" Noah and Sage had given me during our long drives across the country.

"I am." He held a hand out for me to shake. "Thomas Bettencourt, leader of the Bettencourt coven of Chicago —and also the one responsible for saving your life tonight."

I widened my eyes, questions racing through my mind. How did we get to Chicago? At least that's where I assumed we were, although I couldn't tell since all of the curtains in this pristine condo were drawn. And how did Sage and Noah know this vampire? How had he saved my life—and why?

But he seemed like a pretty formal guy, and it looked like he was waiting for me to introduce myself as well. So I'd have to save the questions for later.

"Raven Danvers," I replied, giving his hand a solid shake. He watched me like he wanted more information, so I added, "From LA."

"Nice to officially meet you, Raven Danvers from LA." He released my hand and lowered his arm to his side, the pleasantries apparently over. He'd also sounded a bit suspicious when he'd repeated my name. But I supposed I couldn't blame him.

As I'd learned on this demon hunt, it was highly unusual for a human to travel with—and be protected by—two shifters. It had confused pretty much every supernatural we'd come across so far.

"Thank you for saving my life," I added, and he gave a single nod of acknowledgment. "But what exactly did you do to me? Because I feel… different. I can see things and hear things and smell things that I couldn't before."

"I injected you with my blood." He glanced at a used needle sitting on the coffee table. "As you already knew before coming here, vampire blood has the power to heal humans, even if their injuries are mortal. As a side effect, you'll have vampire abilities for the next twenty-four hours. You'll be staying here until those abilities wear off."

"Oh." It was a lot to take in at once, but there was one bit of what he said that stood out to me the most. "Why do you think I knew vampire blood healed humans before all of this?" I asked. "Because I didn't. Sage and Noah never taught me that during our lessons."

Thomas tilted his head, looking at me with more interest than before. "Fascinating," he said, apparently leaving it at that. "And certainly something to be addressed later. In the meantime, you should know I didn't save your life out of the goodness of my heart. Your friends and I came to an agreement."

Dread swirled in my stomach. "What kind of agreement?" I reached for Noah's hand and grabbed it for support, looking at each of the three of them as I waited for an answer.

Thomas quickly told me about the deal they'd made. The blood oath, the private talk with me, and the date with Sage.

I understood why he wanted us to make the blood oath of silence about vampire blood. I wasn't happy about it—Noah and Sage had explained blood oaths to me, and how I should only enter into one if I had no other option. But I literally had no option right now, since if I didn't make the blood oath, Thomas wasn't going to let me out of this building alive. So it looked like today was the day when I'd be making my first ever blood oath.

I wasn't sure why Thomas wanted to speak privately with me, but there was nothing else I could do but find out.

As for the final condition, I didn't understand why he'd included a date with Sage into the terms while bargaining for my life. He didn't strike me as the type of man who needed to bargain for a date. But looking at the two of them now, there was definitely something between them. He glanced at her every so often with longing in his eyes, and she did the same. Both of them kept looking away from the other before they could get caught.

I'd never pictured Sage being interested in someone so… aloof. But she hadn't said a word since I'd woken up, and I had a feeling that had to do with Thomas.

I'd *definitely* be asking her for the scoop about what was going on between the two of them once we were alone.

"I take it you agree to the terms?" Thomas watched me in challenge. There was an edge to his voice—a warning. That if I didn't agree to the terms, I wasn't going to like the consequences.

"I do." I nodded.

"Good." He stood up. "Then please, come with me. It's time we talk—alone."

I turned to Noah, and he nodded to let me know it was going to be okay. At the same time, a soothing warmth made its way through my body, settling my nerves. While I couldn't say for sure, I could have sworn that the boost of encouragement had radiated from Noah and into me.

I gave his hand a small squeeze—letting him know I got his message—and stood up to go with Thomas. But Thomas didn't continue forward. Instead, he turned around and looked once more at Sage.

"There's a selection of clothes and makeup in the second bedroom." He glanced down the hall to my left— I assumed that was where the second bedroom was. "We'll be leaving for our date after I speak with Raven, so you should take this time to get ready."

Her face paled, and she glanced down the hall, as if deliberately not wanting to make eye contact with Thomas.

I didn't believe this. Sage wasn't afraid of anything. Why did this date have her so on edge?

He didn't wait for her to reply before spinning on his heel and leading the way down the hall.

I looked once more at Sage and Noah. I wanted to stay with them. *Especially* with Noah. I had no idea where things stood between us. Before, he'd told me he wasn't interested in me. But after that kiss when I'd woken up, I knew he'd been lying. He cared for me as much as I cared for him.

We were going to have to talk about it soon.

But not now.

Because according to the terms of the agreement that had saved my life, I had no choice but to follow Thomas down the hall and give him the private audience he'd requested.

9

RAVEN

I FOLLOWED Thomas into a large room that was obviously a media room. The television was bigger than any I'd ever seen—it took up nearly the entire wall it was on.

Actually, calling this a media room was a disservice. It was more like a home theater.

A plush white sofa faced the television, and I walked toward it, unsure if I should sit or stand. I decided to remain standing until seeing what Thomas chose to do.

Thomas closed the door with a resounding click and turned to face me. "Raven Danvers from LA," he said my name like it was some kind of joke, eyeing me up like he'd trapped me. "Or do you prefer to be called Princess Ana of the Seventh Kingdom?"

"What?" I backed away, confused—and also scared. I stumbled into an end table, but my temporarily heightened vampire senses stopped me from falling over and making a total fool of myself.

I rightened myself and looked around. The only way out of the room was from the door Thomas was currently blocking.

"I couldn't be sure given the condition you were in when you arrived," he continued—either not believing my confusion or ignoring it. "You were so burnt that it made you nearly unrecognizable. But now that you're healed, I see my suspicion was correct. So, tell me. What's the infamous Princess Ana of the Seventh Kingdom doing traveling with Sage Montgomery and the First Prophet of the Vale?"

He looked so sure of himself—like he was catching me in a massive lie. Judging by the way he crossed his arms and blocked the door, he didn't want me leaving this room until I confessed.

The problem was, I had nothing to confess *to*.

"I don't know what you're talking about." I leveled my gaze with his, not wanting to let him know how scared I really was. If worst came to worst, I had my temporary vampire strength, and I knew how to defend myself thanks to the lessons Noah had given me. I glanced around for an item I could use as a weapon. A lamp, a glass centerpiece… there were definitely a few items in here I could work with.

"Relax," Thomas said, his eyes dancing in amusement. "If I was going to attack, I would have done it already. And you certainly wouldn't be able to defend yourself against me with a lamp."

My cheeks heated with the realization that he knew exactly what I'd been thinking.

"I don't want to hurt you," he continued. "I just want to talk." He paused to size me up. "Are you ready to answer my questions?"

I took a few deep breaths to center myself. It was clear that Thomas was extremely perceptive and manipulative. But he'd also just saved my life. Surely he wouldn't have saved my life if he wanted to hurt me?

He was also the leader of a vampire coven in one of the biggest cities in America. I had no idea what he was up to, what he wanted, or what he would do to get it.

But there was one thing I *did* know—I didn't have the answers he wanted.

"I can't answer your questions, because I have no idea what you're talking about," I said, the words coming out in a rush. "I don't know who Princess Ana is. I don't know what the Seventh Kingdom is. And I don't know who the First Prophet of the Vale is." I threw my hands up in the air, wishing I could give him more. Then maybe he'd stop looking at me like he thought I was lying scum. "I'm just a human girl who got lucky by being saved by two shifters and now has a chance to save my mom's life. I didn't even believe in the supernatural a month ago." My voice faltered—I was getting desperate now. "I can tell you don't believe me, but it's true. I swear it."

He didn't reply. Instead he just watched me, studying me with eyes that gazed at me like a hawk.

I stood still, afraid to move. Afraid to *breathe*.

After what felt like the longest few seconds of my life, he finally gave me a single nod.

"Very well." He motioned to the couch that faced the television. "Then please, take a seat and allow me to refresh your memory."

10

RAVEN

My *memory.*

Could that be what this was about? My missing memories?

Curious, I sat on the sofa where Thomas was motioning. He did the same, sitting on the opposite end and grabbing a tiny remote from the end table.

The television turned on, and the lights in the room dimmed. Then, a scene on the television started to play.

Thomas hadn't pressed any buttons on the remote—which seemed strange—but I was too stunned by what I saw on the screen to ask any questions.

Because what I saw was… me.

I was barging through the doors of a palace throne room, wearing a long, fancy dress and looking every bit like royalty. There were two people on the throne—a petite woman with long, dark hair and a crown on her head, and a handsome man who looked eerily similar to that famous swimmer who'd died in a hotel bombing in Toronto right before his big Olympic break. I wasn't usually one to follow sports, but photos of those swimmers had been all over the news. His photo had always been shown the most.

In the scene playing in front of me, people lined the sides of the room and gasped when I entered.

"Who are you?" the woman on the throne asked. Her eyes shined with distrust, and everyone quieted as she continued. "Why are you barging into our ceremony unannounced?"

"My name is Princess Ana." I watched as the girl who looked *exactly* like me held onto her skirt and lowered herself into a curtsy. She addressed the man—not the woman who had questioned her. Her eyes didn't leave his as she spoke. "I'm from the Seventh Kingdom, and I'm here to compete for Prince Jacen's hand in marriage."

The scene paused, leaving me looking at a still image of myself. It was beyond eerie to look at. Because it wasn't just that she looked similar to me.

She was *identical* to me.

The lights brightened again, and Thomas turned in my direction. He looked exceedingly proud at himself—

like he'd just bested me in a competition and was ready for me to admit my defeat. "Either you're Princess Ana, or you have an identical twin," he said, studying me. "From the look on your face, I'm starting to wonder if maybe it's the latter."

"I don't have a twin," I said. I'd seen videos of my delivery—my grandparents had been a bit obsessive when it came to documenting my childhood. There was no twin, and twins didn't run in my family. "But that wasn't me," I repeated. "Unless…"

"Unless what?" Thomas didn't move, waiting for me to continue.

"When was that recording from?" I asked.

"Right after the new year," he said. "January third, to be precise."

The moment he said the date, the world stilled around me. Because my suspicion was correct.

That scene I'd just watched had happened during the time that my memories had been erased and replaced.

"You look like you just saw a ghost," Thomas observed, lounging back in the couch like this was a completely normal conversation. "Either that, or you had a startling realization. Care to share what it was?"

Even though he'd asked politely, I could tell I didn't have much of an option—at least not if I planned on leaving this room anytime soon. Plus, he *had* just saved my life. And Sage had trusted him enough to bring me here, and she and Noah had agreed to let me have this talk with Thomas in the first place.

But still, my memory loss was personal. I wasn't sure if I should tell him, or if I did, I wasn't sure how *much* I should tell him.

"You can either be honest with me, or I'll give you truth potion to find out what you know," he continued. "I recommend that you're willfully honest. I know you don't know much about me, but I'm a valuable ally. You want me on your side. But first, I need to know I can trust you." He glanced at the frozen image of me on the screen, and then looked back to me. "Can you help me do that?"

I swallowed and wrung my hands in my lap. He was coercing me—threatening me with telling me he'd just give me truth potion anyway—and I didn't like that. It was cunning and manipulative.

But it had only been a few minutes, and I already had more information about my missing memories than anyone had been able to give me so far. He had recordings of what I'd done during that time. The answers were literally right in front of my face.

I had to tell him. I needed to know the truth. I was the girl in the video, and while I had no idea why I'd pretended to be this Princess Ana of the Seventh Kingdom, I was ready to find out.

"I traveled around Europe for a few weeks this past winter," I began, keeping my gaze steady with his as I spoke. "But the trip never made sense—it wasn't like me to pick up and leave without telling anyone. And the memories of my time there were always hazy, like I was seeing through someone else's eyes and not my own. Which I recently learned means I'd been given a memory potion—one strong enough to erase *weeks* of memories and replace them with others. In my case, a trip to Europe that never happened."

"A human shouldn't have the strength to see through a memory potion strong enough to erase *weeks* of memory," Thomas said. "I can't smell your scent thanks to the cloaking ring you're wearing, but I know you're human. Your body would have rejected my blood otherwise."

"Why?" I asked. Sage and Noah apparently hadn't gotten that far in my supernatural lessons.

"Supernaturals can't drink vampire blood," he answered. "Just like vampires can't drink the blood of other supernaturals. If we try, it makes us sick so we expel the blood. Therefore, I know you're human, since you drank my blood and it healed you. But Princess Ana is a vampire princess. Watch her prove it to Queen

Laila." He glanced back over at the television, and the scene resumed.

I watched as Princess Ana and the petite vampire on the throne beside Prince Jacen—Queen Laila, according to Thomas—discussed the Seventh Kingdom. Queen Laila doubted Princess Ana was who she claimed to be. She didn't believe there was a Seventh Kingdom at all.

Princess Ana proved she could use the royal vampire ability of compulsion by compelling one of the vampire guards to remove his clothing and do a headstand in the center of the room. He removed his pants and his shoes, but Queen Laila used her compulsion—which was stronger than Princess Ana's, since she was a queen—to stop the guard from continuing.

How disappointing. It would have been funny to watch the guard complete Princess Ana's command.

It also would have been very unlike me to prove I could use compulsion by forcing a random guard to embarrass himself. Surely I could have proven myself without making an enemy of one of the vampire guards of the Vale in the process?

Princess Ana might have *looked* identical to me, but she certainly wasn't behaving like me.

What must have happened to me in those weeks I'd forgotten that would have made me act like that?

The possibilities were disturbing, to say the least.

Thomas stopped the recording—I wasn't sure *how,* since I didn't see him press any buttons—and turned back to me. "As you just saw, Princess Ana is a vampire princess," he said. "Now here you are—the same girl—as a human."

"So… you think someone turned me into a vampire princess, then turned me back into a human and erased my memories?" It sounded crazy, but my life had been so crazy recently that I was beginning to just accept it and go with it.

"It's impossible for vampires to turn back into humans, or even to disguise ourselves as humans," he said. "We can use cloaking rings to disguise our scent, but those just hide our scent—they don't make us smell human. Which leads me to believe…" he trailed off, as if trying to decide if his guess was accurate enough to share.

"What?" I sat forward, eager to know his thoughts.

"You must have been drinking the blood of a vampire royal, which would have made you appear—and smell—like a vampire to everyone you encountered," he said.

"Like I did just now, with your blood," I said, and he nodded. "But you said the vampire blood would only stay in my system for twenty four hours."

"It will," he said. "And Princess Ana was in the Vale for much longer than that. Which means—"

"I must have been working with someone," I cut him off, the pieces quickly coming together in my mind. "And that person was able to get me fresh royal vampire blood to drink each day."

11

RAVEN

"Bingo." The corner of Thomas's lip curved up into a small smile. "For a human, you're much quicker to catch onto all of this than I anticipated."

"Apparently I've been through all of this before." I leaned back into the sofa and sighed, purposefully ignoring his jab at my being a human.

"You have," he said. "But I can't imagine which vampire royal would do this, or what their motives would be. It makes no sense."

"Do you have more videos from my time in the Vale?" I asked. "Maybe we'll get answers there."

"I do," he said. "As you saw, this winter Prince Jacen had vampire princesses from the different kingdoms come to the Vale in a competition for his hand in marriage. Queen Laila decided it would be fun to broadcast the competition throughout the Vale—like a reality show. I have footage from all the broadcasts."

"How?" I asked. "I mean, you said it was only broadcasted to the Vale. So how do you have it here, in Chicago?"

His eyes gleamed with mischief. "I have my ways," he answered, clearly not wanting to give any more information than that. "Anyway, Princess Ana made it to the final two in the competition, so she was in it until the end. I have enough footage of her to keep you entertained until the effects of my blood wear off."

"You mean I almost married the prince of the Vale?" I frowned, unable to imagine myself with anyone other than Noah. Despite how attractive Prince Jacen looked in the footage I saw of him, the knowledge that I might have been intimate with him and then had those memories wiped made me feel dirty, like there were bugs crawling all over my skin.

I rubbed my hands over my arms, but it didn't help me feel better.

"Yes." Thomas nodded and rubbed his chin. "I'm not sure what would have happened if Jacen had chosen you. I can only suspect that the vampire royal you were working with had a mission they wanted you to complete in the Vale. The only way to figure out what that mission was is to find out which royal you were working for."

"You'll help me do that?" I asked.

"No." He chuckled and sat back, like I was a pet that had amused him. "It wouldn't benefit me to potentially make an enemy of another royal vampire by sticking my nose in his or her business. This is something you'll have to figure out on your own."

I nodded, my mind already wandering to the many other problems this new revelation could have for me. "Sage, Noah, and I are heading to Avalon," I said slowly, dread creeping into my stomach. "Prince Jacen is there. When he sees me, he'll recognize me. Not as me, but as Princess Ana."

"He will," Thomas said. "As will everyone else in the Vale, which is where you need to go to get vetted and transported to Avalon."

"I'll need to disguise myself." I sat forward, the perfect idea popping into my mind—thanks to everything Sage and Noah had taught me during our drives. "I can take transformation potion before getting to the Vale. Then, once I'm in Avalon, I can reveal myself to Prince Jacen and tell him the truth about everything. I bet he'll want to figure out who was behind this just as badly as I do."

"I'd say so," Thomas said. "It's not a bad plan, little human. Good job."

I huffed—I *hated* when supernaturals called me "human" instead of referring to me by my actual name.

I would have said something to put him in his place if a more important realization hadn't come to me at the same time.

"I'm confused about something," I said instead.

"Given everything you've been through, I'm sure you're confused about many things," he said.

I glared at him, annoyed that he kept talking down to me. Being human didn't make me less than him or any other supernatural, and I wasn't going to let it slide again. "Given what I've been through, *I* think I'm handling everything pretty well," I said, throwing his words right back in his face. "I've done a lot despite having no supernatural abilities. Including slaying a demon with a weapon that nearly killed me, in case you've already forgotten about that."

He said nothing, which I figured was as much of an agreement as I was going to get from him. I also figured it meant I could continue with my question.

"Prince Jacen was holding a competition to choose a vampire princess from another kingdom to marry," I said, returning to where we'd left off. "I came in second place—which means he chose one of the other princesses. But Noah and Sage told me that Jacen's in a relationship with the Earth Angel in charge of Avalon. Annika."

"That's all true," Thomas confirmed.

"So what happened to the vampire princess he chose as his bride?"

"Princess Karina," he said, as if I should recognize the name. I didn't. "She fled from the palace after Annika killed Queen Laila. But I'm sure Noah can tell you far more about her than I can."

"Why?" My stomach swirled. From the dark tone in Thomas's voice, I didn't have a good feeling about where he was going with this.

"Because Noah used to go by another name—the First Prophet of the Vale." From the way Thomas smirked, I had a feeling he'd been waiting to tell me this since getting me into this room. "He lived in the Vale and worked with a powerful witch to lead the wolves there to war against the vampires. When Karina fled the palace, she ran straight into Noah's arms—and she stood by him until the witch cast the spell that opened the Hell Gate and released the demons upon the Earth."

12

RAVEN

"YOU'RE LYING," I said. "Noah *hates* demons. There's no way he would do that."

"Why would I lie about this?" He gave me an innocent look that I was positive meant he was enjoying this.

"I don't know," I said. "But I know Noah. He wants to get to Avalon more than anything, so he can join the Earth Angel's army and defeat the demons for good."

"Are you sure that's why he's going to Avalon?" he asked.

"Why else would he be going to Avalon?" I clenched my fists, getting angry now. Thomas was talking about Noah like he knew him. But he didn't. I was the one who'd been traveling with Noah for over a week. It didn't sound like much, but during that time, we'd barely been apart. Noah was honorable and good.

Despite how frustrating he could be, he'd proven that his heart was in the right place on multiple occasions.

But he was also secretive. He never talked about his past, and whenever I asked him about it, he clammed up.

He was hiding something from me. I couldn't deny it.

But surely it couldn't be something as awful as what Thomas had claimed?

"He could be going so he can take Avalon down from the inside," Thomas casually threw the idea out there, like he wasn't also saying that he thought Noah was a terrible person. "The Earth Angel's army is the best chance we have at defeating the demons. Take down her army, and once the demons strike, they'll be unstoppable."

"Noah wouldn't do that," I insisted. "Destroying the demons is everything to him. And even if you were right —which you aren't—one man couldn't take down the Earth Angel's entire army from the inside. It would be a suicide mission."

"You'd be surprised by what one man can do when he has enough drive to succeed," Thomas said knowingly. "And from what I've heard about the First Prophet, he's quite skilled at influencing those around him. Look at him now—he has you and Sage believing his every word. If he were human, I'd think his ability of influence was a gift from the gods. But as a born shifter, it's simply a honed skill. An impressive skill, but only a skill."

"You're lying," I said again.

Unfortunately, the more Thomas told me, the more I wondered what exactly Noah had been keeping from me. It had to do with where he was from. I knew that much.

But it couldn't be what Thomas had said—about Noah helping a witch open the Hell Gate. That was too awful to think about.

"You don't believe that as strongly as before," he observed.

I narrowed my eyes at him, annoyed at him for reading me so well. "If what you're saying *is* true—which I don't think it is—then it doesn't make any sense," I said, trying to work through this logically. "The demons want to kill all supernaturals—including shifters."

"They do," he confirmed.

"So why would Noah release the demons from Hell when they want to kill his entire species?"

"I don't know." Thomas glanced at his watch. "But I requested this private audience with you because I thought you were Princess Ana. Since your memory has been wiped, there's nothing more I can learn from you now. So it's time I leave for my date with Sage. We'll be gone long enough for you to confront the First Prophet yourself."

"Seriously?" I asked. "You think Noah is this evil First Prophet who released the demons from Hell and is going to Avalon to destroy the Earth Angel's army from the inside, and you're just… letting us hang out in your penthouse?"

"Yep," he said.

"Well, you must not think he's *that* dangerous if you're leaving him alone here," I challenged.

"The Bettencourt is more secure than a prison." He stood up and adjusted a button on his suit jacket. "No one's getting out of here unless I let them out."

"So you're trapping us here." I stood up as well, not wanting to let him tower over me. He was tall, so he still towered over me, but not as much as he would have if I'd remained sitting.

"That's one way of looking at it," he said.

"There's another way?" I didn't bother keeping the sarcasm from my tone.

"There's always more than one way of looking at things," he said. "In this case, it's that I'm keeping you here for your own protection."

"That's a load of crap and you know it." I scoffed. "If we can't leave without your permission, then we're prisoners here, plain and simple."

He watched me for a few seconds, neither of us saying a word. I pressed my lips together, determined not to stand down.

"I like you, Raven," he finally said. "I didn't think I would, but you're fiery. You say what's on your mind. It's refreshing."

I hadn't been expecting that, and the sudden turn of the conversation left me speechless.

"On that note, I'm off on my date with Sage," he said. "Enjoy your time with your boyfriend while we're gone. I'll send him in. You clearly have a lot to discuss."

The door opened without Thomas having to touch it, and he zipped out of the room before I could say another word.

I stared at the open doorway, nervous to see Noah. Up until now, I'd never doubted that he was the good guy. A hero.

But after what Thomas had said, I had an awful feeling that whatever Noah was hiding from me was worse than I'd imagined.

And that maybe the line between good and evil wasn't as clear as it had originally appeared.

13

THOMAS

THE INFORMATION I'd gotten from Raven was fascinating, to say the least. It made me wonder—had a vampire royal been working with the Earth Angel to assassinate Laila, the previous queen of the Vale? The timing of Princess Ana infiltrating the palace and Laila's assassination couldn't have been a coincidence.

With some digging, I could likely get to the bottom of which royal vampire was behind this. Then I could use what I knew to my advantage.

For now, I'd keep the information where it was safest —to myself.

I passed Noah on my way out of the media room. "You're free to go to your girlfriend now," I told him. "She's going to have lots of questions."

Noah nodded and made his way to the room where Raven was waiting.

I couldn't wait to see how *that* discussion would play out. Like everywhere else in the Bettencourt, each room in my penthouse was outfitted with microscopic cameras. I wouldn't be able to watch Noah and Raven's conversation live—I had more important matters to attend to—but I planned on watching the recording later.

For now, I entered my bedroom. When the door shut behind me, I reached for my cell phone to call Flint.

Sage's brother knew that Sage, Noah, and Raven were going to be arriving at the Bettencourt. *How* he knew was another question—one I didn't know the answer to—but he knew. And he'd insisted—no, begged —that once they arrived, I did whatever it took to get Sage back to the Montgomery compound in LA. He'd given me this whole story about how Sage had been brainwashed by the First Prophet into following him on his mission to kill demons, and that if she didn't get back to LA soon, she'd be left out of an important alliance that Flint was making to ensure the safety of the Montgomery pack.

It sounded compelling, especially because I'd do anything to ensure Sage's safety. I'd bring her back to LA myself in a heartbeat if I thought Flint was telling the truth.

There were a bunch of clues that made me suspect he was lying. But mainly, I knew Sage. She wasn't the type to be brainwashed, even by the First Prophet. She was traveling with him for a reason.

I was taking her on our date tonight so I could discover exactly what that reason was.

But first, I needed to talk to her brother.

I waited as the call went through. Every room in my penthouse was equipped with the best sound blocking technology on the market. Some that wasn't even *on* the market yet. No one would be able to hear what I was saying in here—not even a supernatural.

Flint picked up on the third ring.

"You have my sister?" he asked.

"I do," I confirmed. "She came straight to my doorstep, just like you told me."

"Of course she did," Flint said. "My source wouldn't lie."

"What source is that?" I asked casually. Truth be told, I was dying to know what sort of intel Flint had at his disposal. But I knew better than to act like I cared too much, which was why I kept it casual.

"That's for me to know," Flint said. "And for you to *maybe* find out if you get Sage back to LA safely."

It was a good thing this wasn't a video call, because I *needed* to roll my eyes after hearing how childish Flint sounded.

"She only just arrived," I said calmly. "I'm working on it."

"What's there to work on?" He sounded just as erratic as he had the last time we talked. "Can't you just drug her, stick her on that plane of yours, and have her here in a few hours?"

I frowned at the notion of drugging Sage and sending her anywhere against her will.

The fact that Flint wanted me to do that to her made me question again what he was truly up to.

"Be patient," I said. "You told me you had a week until you needed her back. If you want her to come to you willingly—which you should, since Sage can hold one hell of a grudge—you'll let me do this my way."

"Once Sage is back, she won't care how she got here —she'll just be grateful she's safe." Flint growled. "You better stick to your promise to get her home. You'll regret it if you don't."

"Are you threatening me?" The question was rhetorical—he obviously was. And I had no intention of letting him think I was going to let that fly.

"If you don't bring Sage to me within a week, I'll be

forced to go through with this alliance without her, due to a blood oath I made," he said. "If that happens, Sage won't be safe and the demons will come for her sooner rather than later."

"You're not making sense, Flint." If I was a less patient man, I might have lost my temper on him by now. "What do the demons want with Sage?"

"Once I've made this alliance, the demons will hear of it," he said darkly. "They'll go after any member of the Montgomery pack who remains unprotected. If Sage isn't protected, she'll be first on their hit list since she's so close to me."

"Sage is protected," I said, since I'd do anything to keep her safe—even if that meant giving up everything I'd built here in Chicago and going with her to the Haven. "Or do you doubt me that much?"

"If I doubted you, I wouldn't have come to you," he said. "Speaking of, how's it going with the First Prophet and his pet human? I assume they're already taken care of?"

"I'm in the process of it as we speak," I said.

"How is that not done already?" Flint growled again. "The First Prophet is dangerous. He should have been killed immediately."

"You must not know me if you think I'd kill anyone

before squeezing all the information out of them that I can." I chuckled. "They'll be handled soon. No need to worry about that."

"Don't take too long," he said. "And don't underestimate them. The longer they're there, the more chances they'll have to escape."

"The only person who decides who comes and goes from here is me," I said. "They sealed their fates the moment they walked through my doors."

"True, true," Flint agreed. "Kill them at your convenience. But bring Sage to me before the week is up. If you don't you'll regret it."

He hung up, and I stared at my phone in shock.

I was doing Flint a favor by getting Sage back home. Who did he think he was by hanging up on me?

My initial urge was to call him back, tell him just that, and call off our agreement.

But I took a deep breath, centering myself. Giving into emotional urges might feel good in the moment, but I didn't get to where I was today by acting on impulses. I had to stay in control. Sage's involvement in this stirred up emotions I wasn't used to feeling, but control would allow me to play the long game and come out on top.

So I set my phone to the side. After all, I had a date to get ready for.

And alone time with Sage Montgomery would be the perfect opportunity to talk with her and determine who to believe in this situation—Sage, or Flint.

I knew which one of them I wanted to trust.

Now, all I could do was hope she proved me right.

14

SAGE

After Thomas had left to talk with Raven, I'd told Noah that I didn't have to get ready for the date yet. I'd sit with him and wait to make sure Raven was okay.

He'd insisted I go ahead and get ready. Apparently he wanted the time alone to think and to prepare for telling Raven about their imprint bond. I also needed time to think—being around Thomas had affected me in ways I was hoping it wouldn't—so I was happy to take some much needed alone time.

I knew the way to the second bedroom. I knew my way around the entire Bettencourt hotel.

Growing up, Flint had sent me to Chicago for a few weeks each summer to solidify our alliance with the Bettencourt coven. In return, Thomas had sent his most cherished vampire—a cousin he'd found and turned—to stay in the Montgomery compound. It was abnormal for vampires and shifters to work together, so this was an exercise in trust to show we had faith in our alliance. By the leader of each group sending their closest family member to the other's territory for a few weeks each summer, it showed that we trusted that the Montgomerys and the Bettencourts would always keep one another safe.

Thomas's idea, of course.

I'd started coming here when I was twelve. At first, I'd stayed in a private guest suite. Those initial summers had been lonely, since the Bettencourt vampires weren't particularly interested in spending time with a twelve year old. So I was constantly exploring the hotel and getting into all kinds of trouble.

The other vampires had scolded me, but Thomas always seemed amused by my antics. He also always made sure I had enough games, movies, books, and such to keep me entertained. He'd even set aside nights to take me out of the city so I could change into my wolf form and run.

Our relationship wasn't romantic when I'd been so young, but I'd had a crush on him and knew I trusted him. I think that time he spent with me when I was young allowed him to feel freer than he allowed himself to be when he was at the Bettencourt, responsible for the safety of his entire coven.

We started dating the summer when I was sixteen. I'd gotten a car a few months earlier, and that had been the start of my "rebellious phase," as Flint liked to call it. Honestly, I don't think that phase ever ended, but whatever.

The moment I'd arrived at the Bettencourt that summer, Thomas had looked at me differently.

He'd looked at me the way a man looks at a woman he's attracted to, instead of like a kid he has to take care of.

The tension between us grew like a wildfire. The first night he took me out to run that summer, I was quick to kiss him and show him that his feelings were returned.

In that instant, everything between us *clicked*. Like we were meant to be.

After that night, I switched from staying in the guest suite to staying in the second bedroom in his penthouse.

He didn't allow me to stay with him in his room until I was eighteen. Because of that, much of the time that I'd spent in the Bettencourt had been in the bedroom I was heading to now.

The room was exactly as I remembered it. Furniture in shades of gray, an upholstered bed that I knew was heavenly to sleep in, mirrored nightstand and lamps, and a crystal chandelier fit for a princess. Normally, the curtains were open to a spectacular view of the city, but like all the shades throughout the penthouse right now, they were currently closed.

The remote to control the curtains was inside the top drawer of the nightstand closest to the window, exactly as I remembered. But when I pressed the button to open them, they remained closed.

Someone who didn't know Thomas might have chalked it up to faulty technology. But I knew him, and I knew that the remote didn't work because he either didn't want us seeing outside, or he didn't want to risk anyone outside seeing in. I suspected the latter. I tossed the control back into the drawer, knowing it wouldn't work until Thomas deemed it safe to open the curtains.

Then I took my time in the luxurious shower, cleaning off all the dirt and grime from fighting that red-eyed wolf shifter in the alley in Nashville. I still had no idea what that creature was. I should have been thinking about it—trying to figure out why a shifter had the red eyes of a demon.

Instead, all I could think about was Thomas.

Being in this room where I'd spent time with him brought back memories I wished would remain buried.

Now, as I scrubbed myself clean, all the memories came to the surface again.

Especially one in particular, from the final night I spent here during the summer when I was sixteen.

———

I was zipping up my final suitcase, preparing to head back to LA in the morning. As much as I hated it, I cried the entire time I'd packed. I hated seeing my stuff all packed up—I hated knowing that soon, this incredible summer with Thomas would only be a memory.

Suddenly, the door opened. Thomas. His jacket and tie were off, and the sleeves of his button-down top were pushed up to his elbows. He watched me with tortured sadness—like he was seeing me for the last time.

He'd been looking at me like that a lot the past few days. Like I was going away and never coming back.

"You're crying." He tilted his head, watching me in that curious way of his—like he was studying me and trying to figure out how my emotions worked. He always ended up asking. I wasn't one of his machines or political alliances, and I apparently surprised him more than he liked to admit. "Why?"

"I don't want to leave here." I wiped a tear from my eyes

and forced a smile, despite feeling as far from happy as ever. "I don't want to leave you."

"I don't want you to leave, either." He took a few steps forward and stopped, looking like he wasn't sure if he should come closer or keep his distance. "I'd keep you here—with me—if I could."

I smirked, a crazy idea popping into my mind. Instead of saying it immediately, I rushed over to Thomas and wrapped my arms around his neck, bringing his lips down to mine.

He didn't fight me. He never did.

I deepened the kiss and pushed my body against his, smiling when he let out a tortured groan. Thomas was always so calm and in control—I loved being the only one who could get him to let down his guard.

I eventually broke the kiss and smiled in mischief. "You're the leader of the Bettencourt coven," I said, my gaze locked on his. "You can do anything you want."

"Not anything," he said reluctantly. "I love you Sage, but if your brother knew about what happened between the two of us this summer..." He let the thought hang, although I was barely focused on what he was saying anymore. "I don't think he'd ever let you leave the Montgomery compound again. He certainly wouldn't let you anywhere near me."

"You love me?" I stared up at him as I waited for him to confirm that he meant it—that I wasn't just hearing what I'd been hoping he would say for weeks. Years, if I was being honest with myself.

"Of course I love you," he said. "I loved you since the first summer I took care of you, but this summer, that love changed. It grew. I'm in love with you, Sage Montgomery. You're the most fascinating, beautiful, infuriating woman I know, and I'm so madly in love with you that I can't think straight anymore. It's driving me crazy. Before this ends—before you leave here—I needed you to know that."

"Who said anything about this ending?" My heart dropped at the thought of it. He couldn't say something so amazing and then imply we were over. It didn't make any sense.

"I know how shifter biology works." He pulled away, his eyes flashing with pain. "You're going to be back home, among others of your kind, for months. If you imprint on any of them while you're there, I won't blame you for choosing your potential mate over me. Your happiness is more important to me than anything. I'd want you to choose him over me."

"Never," I said stubbornly. "Since you know how shifter biology works, then you know I have to kiss another shifter to imprint on them. Which isn't going to happen. Because I love you too, Thomas Bettencourt. And the only lips I want to kiss are yours."

I shut off the water in the shower, the memory feeling like it had just happened yesterday. Right after telling him I loved him, I'd pulled him to me again. That kiss hadn't ended nearly as quickly as the previous one.

The Thomas from all those years ago was so different from the cold, hardened man I saw today.

A huge part of me wanted to run up to him like I had back then and kiss him with that same wild abandonment—like I was young, in love, and without a care in the world. I wanted to break down his walls in the way he'd once told me only I was able to do.

I wanted to go back to the time before he'd ruined everything.

But I couldn't. Because if he'd truly loved me as much as he'd claimed, he wouldn't have broken our engagement. He wouldn't have gone *years* without contacting me—as if I never mattered to him at all.

I'd just been a game to him. Another one of his machines to study, play with, and master.

Once I'd said yes to his proposal, he'd tossed me aside like a piece of old technology.

And nothing he might say to me on this date could ever make me forget that.

15

SAGE

THE CLOSET WAS FILLED with women's clothing, and the bathroom stocked with hair supplies and makeup.

Why did Thomas have all that stuff in his penthouse?

Jealously burned at the pit of my stomach at the thought of another woman here, in the room that had been mine. Obviously I knew Thomas was likely seeing people after breaking our engagement, but actually seeing evidence of it hurt more than I cared to admit.

He had another woman living with him, and here I was—a defective shifter who had yet to imprint on anyone. I felt like such a loser. This all would have been so much easier if I'd come to him for help and had a sexy shifter mate by my side who I was hopelessly in love with. But no. I was forever cursed to be alone.

But I refused to let Thomas get to me. I was here for

Raven—not for me. I'd agreed to this date for *Raven*.

Plus, just because I'd agreed to go on a date with him didn't mean I had to dress like I cared what happened on the date. Especially considering that Thomas had a woman living in this room, which meant he shouldn't be *going* on a date with his ex-fiancée at all.

This was messed up on so many levels.

I browsed through the clothes in the closet, determined to find the most casual outfit possible. All of the clothes were in my style, which definitely weirded me out a bit. Apparently, Thomas had a type.

I considered putting on the same clothes I wore when I got here, but they were dirty and smelly. While that would get across the message that this date meant nothing to me, I'd just gotten out of the shower, and the prospect of putting my dirty clothes on again wasn't appealing at all.

Proving a point didn't mean I had to be gross.

So I put on the most casual clothes I found amongst all the dresses and fancy tops—jeans and a black tank.

I wasn't going to put on any makeup, since if I did, it would look like I cared. But the circles under my eyes were atrocious, so I dabbed some concealer on them. The purpose of concealer was to look natural, and guys didn't know enough about makeup to realize I was wearing it, anyway.

All the makeup in the drawer was unused. And the concealer matched my skin tone perfectly.

Strange.

I threw my wet hair up into a ponytail—the least sexy thing I could think to do with it. Nothing said, "I don't care if you think I look hot or not" like a wet, messy ponytail.

I gave myself a once-over in the mirror. I looked ready for a girls' night in. Perfect.

I opened the door to return to the living room. But Thomas was already standing outside, preparing to knock.

His eyes widened, and he took a step back. "Sage." He straightened and cleared his throat. "I was just coming by to see if you were ready to leave."

If he thought I didn't look ready, he said nothing.

Ugh. So frustrating.

Even more frustrating was that he was dressed casually—for him—too. Slacks and a white button down top.

He knew I thought he looked hot in white button down tops.

What kind of game was he trying to play with me?

"I'm ready." I marched past him, refusing to let him take the lead—and not wanting him to see the effect he had on me. "Let's get this over with."

16

SAGE

THOMAS LED me up to the roof of the Bettencourt, where a helicopter waited for us.

"Always such a show off." I glared at the helicopter and rolled my eyes.

The light in his eyes dimmed, like my reaction had been a punch in the gut. Good. "You love the helicopter," he said.

That was back when I loved you.

The words were on the tip of my tongue, but I didn't say them. I couldn't bring up my feelings for him. If I did, I didn't trust myself not to burst into tears.

"That was a long time ago," I said instead.

"Something happened between then and now that caused this intense aversion to helicopters?" he teased.

This time I glared at him—not at the helicopter. He

had no right to act casual and friendly after what he did to me. And if he thought I was going to go along with it, he was terribly mistaken.

"Cut the crap," I said. "I agreed to go on this date with you, but I didn't agree to forgive you. Pretending like everything's fine between us isn't going to make what you did to me go away."

A myriad of emotions crossed his face. He eventually settled on his typical detached look. "Noted." He walked over to the helicopter and held the door open for me. All traces of friendliness were gone from his tone. "Hurry up inside, then. The sooner you get in, the faster we can get this over with."

The helicopter ride passed in silence. Thomas piloted, and I gazed out the windows, watching as the city skyscrapers gave way to suburbs, and eventually gave way to nothing. It took everything in me not to press my hands against the windows and stare out in awe like I did when I was sixteen.

Eventually, Thomas made a sharp turn, and we headed over Lake Michigan.

I sat back and swallowed, knowing exactly where we were going.

The private island Thomas owned and had taken me to many times during my summers here.

When I was twelve, he'd taken me there to prove he owned an island. Twelve-year-old me had been extremely impressed. I'd thought he was a king, and that the island was a magical land where anything could happen, like the ones from storybooks.

When I was sixteen, he'd taken me there so I could shift into my wolf form and run freely through the woods. We'd kissed for the first time on that island.

When I was seventeen, he'd taken me there and we'd sat out on the beach talking for hours. We'd fantasized about living there, just the two of us together, with no one else in the world to bother us. I'd even planned out our perfect dream house, complete with a dock and a boat.

When I was eighteen, he'd taken me there, gotten on one knee, and asked me to marry him. That had been the happiest moment of my life.

It still *was* the happiest moment of my life, if I was being honest with myself.

How pathetic was I, that my happiest moment was when the man who had broken my heart had proposed to me years ago?

The island came into sight, and I saw lights on it. Those were new. Despite owning the island, Thomas had never built anything on it. He'd left it natural and wild—his own personal escape from the busy world he lived in.

As we got closer, the thing he'd built on the island came into view.

It was a house. And it wasn't just any house. It was a beautiful castle-like home with a dock leading out to a boat on the lake.

It was the house from my dreams. From *our* dreams.

He landed us in the yard, and I stared out at the house as he powered the helicopter off.

"You built it," I said once the helicopter went silent. "The house we talked about that summer. You *built* it."

I couldn't believe it. This felt like a dream—not like real life.

"I did," he said.

I turned toward him, tears brimming my eyes. "Why?"

"It was going to be an engagement present." He looked out to the house, staring at it with wistfulness and longing.

Like he was longing for something he'd never have.

I touched the finger on my left hand, as if imagining the ring I'd once wore was still there. None of this made any sense. Why would he build our dream house and plan on giving it to me as an engagement present if he didn't want to marry me? Why was he bringing me here now? And why did he look just as heartbroken as I felt?

It was too much at once. I needed air.

I opened the door of the helicopter and jumped out of it, walking toward the house. I heard Thomas do the same, and he followed behind me.

Eventually I stopped in front of the sidewalk and stared up at the house. It was exactly what we'd planned, down to the turret with a tower that looked out toward the lake.

"Tell me what you're thinking," Thomas said from next to me. "Not knowing is killing me."

"You wanted me to come on this date with you because you wanted my forgiveness," I said, reminding him about his claim from earlier. He nodded, and I continued, "But showing me this house isn't going to magically make everything better. I can't forgive you if you never explain why you did it to me. Why you..." I paused, getting in control of myself to make sure I didn't start crying while saying it. "Why you broke our engagement and stopped talking to me, kicking me out of your life like you never loved me at all."

"After everything we went through, you think I never loved you?" His eyes flashed with pain, like my words had physically hurt him.

I was glad for it. I'd suffered so much—it was gratifying to see that he might feel some of that pain, too. "You broke our engagement and stopped talking to me." I glared up at him. "What was I supposed to think?"

"You're right," he admitted.

"Really?" I was shocked—those were words Thomas didn't speak often. "About which part?"

"All of it," he said, and I stilled, bracing myself for what was coming next. "I just thought if I broke it off quickly, it would be less painful. That you'd be able to move on faster."

I said nothing, since what was there to say? Admitting the truth—that I'd *never* moved on—was too pathetic. Instead, I stayed silent. A warm summer breeze blew up at us from the lake, and I took a deep breath, loving the familiar, earthy smell of the island. The moon was only a tiny sliver in the sky, and at this time of night so far from the city, it was easy to believe we were the only two people in the world.

It was also easy to believe we were the people we once were. But I steered my mind from that path, not willing to let it go there.

"I was wrong, and I see that now." He watched me with so much sadness—like he wanted to put together the broken pieces of my heart.

Deep down, I wished he could. But it was too late for that.

"I'm sorry," he added.

"You were definitely wrong." I crossed my arms, still unable to accept his apology. "And while it's nice to hear you admit it, I can't forgive you."

"Why not?" He spun to face me, looking angry now. "I'm doing everything I can to show you I'm sorry. I built our house. I saved your friend's life. I told you I was wrong breaking it off the way I did. What else do you want from me?"

The intense way he was looking at me took my breath away. But I took a step back, somehow managing to center myself.

"Simple," I said. "I want to know *why* you decided you didn't want to marry me. And the explanation better be good."

Even then, I wasn't sure I'd be able to forgive him.

But at least it would be a start.

17

SAGE

"ALL RIGHT," Thomas said, motioning toward the house. "Do you want to go inside?"

He was stalling.

But I also *really* wanted to see the inside of the house.

"Only if once we get inside, you tell me why you broke off our engagement," I said.

Thomas nodded and led the way inside. I followed, stepping through the front door and into a foyer that looked like it was straight from a fairytale. Every bit of the decoration was traditional and ornate—the exact opposite of Thomas's modern penthouse.

"Wow." I took a few more steps into the hall, letting my fingers linger on the carvings on the wooden entry table. "You really went all out on this."

"The designer did most of the work." He shrugged,

like it was nothing. "But it was what you said you wanted so… here it is."

I nodded, since it was *exactly* the type of decor we'd discussed that summer, when this miniature castle was a fantasy and not something I thought Thomas actually intended on building.

Even though I was inside it right now, it was still hard to believe this was real.

He led the way into the dining room, where the grand wooden table was set for two. "I took the liberty of having dinner ready for us when we arrived." He reached for one of the chairs and pulled it out, motioning for me to sit. "Porterhouse steak, cooked rare, just how you like it. With mac and cheese on the side. And some creamed spinach, in case you want to attempt to be healthy."

"Creamed spinach isn't healthy," I said instantly.

"I know." He smiled. "But it's the only way to get you to eat your vegetables."

My stomach rumbled, and I wrapped my arms around it in embarrassment. I couldn't lie and say I wasn't hungry even if I wanted to. Which I didn't. It had been forever since I'd sat down to a decent meal, and my mouth was already watering at the thought of a perfect, juicy steak.

Hopefully Thomas intended on explaining why he'd

broken our engagement during dinner. Even if he didn't, I was going to insist he did.

But first, food.

"There's staff in the house?" I looked around, expecting a maid or chef to come around the corner at any moment.

"Nope." He smirked. "We're the only ones here. The meal is thanks to the robotic kitchen I had installed. Make yourself comfortable, and I'll bring everything out."

I sat down and placed my napkin on my lap. Of *course* Thomas had a robotic kitchen. I wouldn't have expected anything else.

He used his vampire speed to whiz between the dining room and the kitchen, bringing out a bottle of wine, a carafe of blood, and both of our meals. He poured my wine first, then poured half as much into his glass. He topped the rest of his off with blood.

It took all of my self-control not to dig into my steak the moment he placed it in front of me. But I resisted, since I was a shifter—not a savage.

"A toast." He raised his wineglass in the air. "To finally being reunited after all these years."

"How about a toast to you telling me why you broke our engagement and ignored me for all these years?" I sat back and crossed my arms. If he thought I was going to forget he owed me an explanation because he had my favorite meal waiting, he had another thing coming.

"I thought we might enjoy our dinner first," he said.

"You thought wrong." I took a sip of the wine—delicious, of course—and set it down. Then I picked up my utensils and began cutting into my steak. "Start talking. Now."

He also sipped his wine, looking contemplative as he stared into the glass.

I dug into my steak, determined not to speak again until he offered me an explanation. It oozed with blood, just how I liked it. Delicious. I was more than happy to devour it until Thomas decided to speak. So that was exactly what I did.

Finally, he placed his wineglass down and began. "I loved you, Sage," he said. "I still do. I wanted to marry you more than anything. But marrying you would be selfish. You were so young—you still are. It was my job to be the adult and make the responsible decision to let you go."

I finished chewing, placed my utensils down, and blinked away tears. "I don't understand." I said, trying to swallow down my sadness with another sip of wine. "I loved you. According to what you said just now, you loved me. So why would marrying me be selfish?"

"Because you're a shifter." His voice raised, and he

watched me with such intensity that I could barely move. "I'm a vampire. I know you want to believe that love conquers all, but in real life it doesn't work like that. There are too many differences between our species for marriage to ever work with us.

"There aren't." I glared at him, anger blazing in my chest.

"There are," he insisted.

"Is this about you being immortal?" I asked. "Because you said you didn't care about that. You said you loved me no matter what, and that my physical age didn't matter."

"I meant it," he said. "While that difference would certainly lead to challenges as you aged, it isn't why I ended our engagement."

"Then what is?" I was getting sick of him beating around the bush—he needed to be out with it already.

"Every shifter has a mate," he said darkly. "By marrying you, I'd be stealing you of yours."

"You wouldn't be *stealing* me from anything," I retorted. "You weren't forcing me to marry you. You asked, and I said yes. It was my choice. And I chose you."

"You were eighteen," he said. "You didn't know what you wanted."

"I *did* know what I wanted." I crossed my arms, as if holding them over my chest could stop my heart from hurting. "But even if I didn't, it wasn't your decision to make for me."

"I had just as much of a right to break the engagement as you had a right to say yes when I asked," he said.

"Maybe so," I said. "But not in the way you did. Ignoring my calls, ignoring my texts, refusing to see me when I came to the hotel—you acted like you *hated* me. Do you have any idea how awful that made me feel?"

"I have a bit of an idea," he said. "I read your texts."

"You read them and you didn't care." I stared him down, daring him to contradict me.

"You're wrong." He held my gaze so intensely, like he was speaking straight from his soul. "I did care. More than you'll ever know."

"Then why didn't you act like it?"

"I already told you," he said. "I was protecting you."

"Yeah, right." I shook my head, unable to believe this. If that was protecting me, he had a *very* different definition of the word than I did. "If you loved me, you wouldn't have ignored me. Then I came here for help and you manipulated me into this stupid date. I don't know what kind of game you're trying to play, but I'm not falling for it. Not again."

The words hung in the air, and we stared at each other, saying nothing.

Apparently, we'd reached a standstill.

"It wasn't supposed to be like this," he said sadly. "You were supposed to have found a mate by now. Then you would have understood why I did what I did. You probably would have even thanked me for letting you go. Because my letting you go had allowed you to find him."

"You might be a powerful vampire, but you're definitely not a psychic," I said bitterly. "Because I don't think I *have* a mate. I've never imprinted on anyone."

Shock passed over his face, then doubt. "Have you tried?" he asked.

"I tried." I smirked, hoping what I said next hurt him. "Once I realized you weren't going to talk to me ever again, I was more determined than ever to find my mate. I was so convinced that finding them was the only way to heal my heart that I must have kissed every shifter in the state. But it never happened. By my age, every shifter has at least imprinted on *one* person by now. But not me. Apparently I'm destined to be alone forever."

I'd hoped it would hurt him. Instead, it just sounded pathetic.

That was me. A big, ugly ball of pathetic that repelled anyone I was ever interested in dating.

I wished I could disappear into the floor so I wouldn't have to look at his disappointment for a moment longer. With my food, of course. My love life might be nonexistent, but at least food was always there for me.

"Maybe you're not destined to imprint yet." He sounded way more convinced about it than he had a right to, considering it was my life and not his. "Maybe you aren't meant to find your mate until you get to Avalon."

I backed away from him, immediately suspicious. Because since arriving to the Bettencourt, I hadn't spoken a word about Avalon. Neither had Noah. I wasn't even sure if I was *going* to Avalon. Yes, I was helping Noah and Raven get there, but going to Avalon meant leaving my pack. I didn't think I could do that.

How did Thomas know about Avalon? Could he have motives in bringing me here that went beyond wanting my forgiveness? Could he be working with the Earth Angel... or with Azazel?

I doubted the latter, but who knew how much he'd changed in the past few years? I certainly wasn't the same person I was back then. Why should I expect the same from him?

"I never mentioned Avalon," I said cautiously, not wanting to give too much away. "What do you know about it?"

"When I spoke with Raven privately, she told me she

was heading there," he said simply. "I figured you and Noah were going as well."

"Oh." I took another bite of my food, feeling like an idiot for jumping to the conclusions I did. Of course Thomas wasn't working with Azazel.

He might be cold and dangerous, but he wasn't evil. Well, what he'd done to my heart was pretty evil. But just because he'd dumped me didn't mean he would team up with demons.

At least, I didn't *think* he would team up with demons.

"And your journey to Avalon isn't the most interesting thing I know." He eyed me up, waiting for my reaction.

I didn't give him one. "Care to inform me what is?" I asked, even though I could tell from his tone that he was going to.

"I have eyes everywhere, Sage," he said. "And I know that Noah isn't an average lone wolf. He's the First Prophet of the Vale."

18

SAGE

I FROZE, unsure what to say.

The First Prophet—Noah—had played a huge part in opening the Hell Gate that had released the demons onto Earth. But he and the other shifters had been under the influence of a demon when they'd done what they did. The supernaturals that had been at the war in the Vale knew that.

But supernaturals throughout the world weren't as understanding. Many of them thought Noah should be killed for what he did. It was why he'd been going under the radar for so long. And even though Noah was a common enough name for male shifters, it was part of the reason why we'd originally taken to using fake names on hunts.

"Noah can be trusted," I told Thomas. "He's on our side. He—more than anyone—wants to fight the demons until every last one of them has been wiped off the face of the Earth."

"He's the one who released them from Hell in the first place," Thomas said.

"Not on purpose." I sat straighter, determined to set him right. "He was being manipulated by a demon. He thought he was releasing the wolves' Savior—not opening a Hell Gate."

"Maybe he truly did think he was releasing some mythical Savior." Thomas took another sip of his wine, like we were having a light conversation instead of discussing the beginning of the end of the world. "But no matter how you spin it, he led packs of wolves to murder innocent vampires."

"The vampires of the Vale were hardly innocent," I said, since Thomas knew this as well as anybody. "They kept humans as slaves. They turned humans into vampires against their will. The Vale was a corrupt and brutal place. Don't say otherwise, because I know you agree. You've told me as much yourself."

"All the vampire kingdoms—except for the Haven—are corrupt and brutal places," Thomas said. "Their kings and queens are stuck in the old ways. But that doesn't give a bunch of evangelical wolves the right to march upon the city and murder all the vampires that live there."

I stared at him, feeling like I barely knew him. "When did you get to be so noble?" I asked. "Other than Mary with the Haven, you hate the way the vampire kings and queens run their kingdoms. I thought you would have been happy that Laila was taken down."

"Oh, I *am* happy that Laila was taken down." He raised his glass in a toast. "But the Earth Angel killed Laila *before* the wolves marched upon the city. The wolves had nothing to do with Queen Laila's demise. Their attack wasn't about wanting to hold a coup. It was about murdering all the vampires that lived in the Vale, plain and simple. And the First Prophet played a large role in that."

"Noah tried to stop it," I said. "He went to Prince Jacen to make a deal with him."

"And how did that turn out?" Thomas raised an eyebrow, like he already knew the answer to the question.

"But by that point, everything was already set into motion." I spoke faster now, needing him to understand. Noah's life depended on it. "Noah couldn't stop the wolves from marching upon the city—they were out of his control. But because of his deal with Prince Jacen, the citizens of the Vale had warning about what was coming. They were given the opportunity to escape. Many of them did. The ones who didn't... well, they stayed there by choice. But Noah wanted them all to leave. He didn't want anyone to have to die."

Thomas didn't look convinced. "You speak of the First Prophet fondly," he said, not breaking my gaze. "Are you sure you don't have feelings for him?"

"You mean romantic feelings?" I asked.

"Precisely."

"I'm sure." I laughed. It was tempting to remind him that I hadn't had feelings for anyone since he'd broken my heart, but there was no need to bring *that* up again. "Noah's like a brother to me. I trust him with my life."

"Strong words from a shifter who already has a brother and a pack," he said. "What did the First Prophet do to earn your trust?"

It didn't go beyond my notice that Thomas refused to call Noah by his given name. Thomas didn't trust Noah. Given Noah's history, I couldn't blame him. But Noah was currently in Thomas's penthouse, which meant he was at Thomas's mercy. To ensure his safety, I had to convince Thomas to trust him too.

"I met Noah at an underground shifter bar in LA," I started, thinking back to when I first saw him at that bar. He'd looked so sad and lonely. And haunted. I'd never forget that dark, haunted look he'd had in his eyes that night. "He told me he'd come from the Vale, so I assumed he was one of the many wolves who'd suffered in the war up north. He eventually told me that he was on a mission from the Earth Angel herself—that he had to kill ten demons and present their teeth to her to gain entrance to Avalon. He'd killed his first demon about a week earlier, but he didn't know where to go from there. He had no money, no connections, nothing. He was living on the streets. I felt awful for him—"

"Of course you did," Thomas interrupted.

"What do you mean by that?" I asked.

"Nothing." He smirked. "Just that you have a weakness for strong men in need of your help."

"I fell for you, and you never needed my help," I pointed out.

He cut a piece of his steak, chewed, and swallowed, his eyes distant the entire time. "I needed your help in ways you didn't realize," he said. "But go on. How did you help the First Prophet?"

I wanted to ask Thomas what help he'd needed from me, but there was too much at stake to get distracted right now. I'd come back to it later. For now, I had to get back to convincing him not to kill Noah.

"I took him to the Devereux mansion and paid for

Amber to do a tracking spell to find another demon," I said. "The closest one she could locate was in San Francisco. Noah didn't know how to get there, so I offered to take him."

"Flint was okay with that?" Thomas asked.

"Flint's my brother, not my keeper." I rolled my eyes. "And the Montgomerys don't have any enemies in California. And I definitely lied and told him I was going up there to see a friend. Which wasn't a total lie, because I *did* stop by to see that friend. Just not until after helping Noah kill the demon."

Despite everything, amusement flickered across Thomas's face. "All right," he said. "So, you helped the First Prophet kill one demon. How'd it get from that to you becoming his partner for the rest of his hunt?"

"I couldn't just leave him on his own," I said. "He had no money, no car, no ID—when I said he had nothing, I meant it. He'd lived his whole life in the wilderness of the Vale. There was no record of his entire existence. He needed a leg up. So when we got back to LA I connected him with someone who got him a fake ID, and I had enough cash laying around to buy him a motel room for a week. It was no Ritz-Carlton, but it was better than sleeping on the streets."

"He's the First Prophet." Thomas stared at me like I'd lost my mind. "Not a stray dog."

"He's a good hearted shifter who was in a bad situation, on a mission to join a noble cause." I raised my chin, determined for Thomas to understand. "I wish I could have gotten him something nicer than that motel, but Flint checks my credit card bill each month, so I had to use cash. Luckily, it didn't end up being an issue for much longer," I continued. "Because the next demon we hunted down was in San Diego, and that one didn't go *nearly* as smoothly as the first. Long story short—Noah ended up saving my life."

"Ah," Thomas said. "The good old shifter life debt."

"Yep," I said. "By saving my life, Noah made himself an ally of the Montgomery pack. So I brought him back to the Montgomery compound."

"Just like that?" Thomas's eyes bugged out, apparently thinking I was both crazy *and* stupid.

"He saved my life," I said. "I trusted him."

"You trust too easily," he replied. "I know he saved your life, but what if everything else he said was a lie? What if he was never given the quest to kill ten demons? What if he stole the quest—and the heavenly weapon he's using to kill the demons—from someone else in an attempt to get to Avalon and take it down from the inside?"

I blinked, needing a moment to take in what he'd said. "That's one hell of a conspiracy theory," I finally said. "Not only is it ridiculously far-fetched, but it's also completely wrong."

"It's not far-fetched, given that this is the First Prophet of the Vale we're talking about," Thomas said. "You should have been more careful."

"When I asked Flint if Noah could stay in the pool house, Flint said the same exact thing," I said. "Which was why he only let Noah stay there *after* Noah took a truth potion to confirm his story. So he did, and that was when it came out about his being the First Prophet. We were all shocked, to say the least. But the most shocking of all was that Flint agreed to let him stay with us until finishing his hunt."

"Of course he did." Thomas didn't look shocked in the slightest. "You know how your brother thinks. Keep your friends close, and your enemies closer."

"Noah isn't our enemy." I was determined to have Thomas understand this by the time this meal was over. If he didn't... well, I didn't know how I could help Noah if Thomas decided he wasn't to be trusted.

Thomas was more powerful than the two of us combined.

"Maybe 'enemy' is too harsh of a term," he said. "But the First Prophet is a wild card. Flint wanted him at the Montgomery complex so he could know what he was up to at all times."

"Maybe," I said, since he was right—that sounded just like my brother. "But you should have heard Noah when he told us about everything that happened at the Vale. He was deceived more than anyone. Now he's determined to join the Earth Angel's army and clean up the mess he unintentionally created when that Hell Gate opened. Making this right means everything to him."

"Or so he said…" Thomas mused.

"He took truth potion," I reminded him. "He couldn't have lied if he'd wanted to."

"He's a strong supernatural," Thomas said. "You know how truth potion works. If a supernatural has stronger magic than the witch who created the potion, they can resist it."

"We gave him truth potion brewed by Amber," I said. "The only supernaturals who would be able to resist that would be the original vampires, and *maybe* a few alpha pack leaders."

"And maybe the First Prophet of the Vale," Thomas said with a smirk.

"Ugh." I cut into my steak to get out my frustration. All this talking was making my food get cold. "Noah can be trusted. But of course it would kill you to just trust my instincts about him, wouldn't it? Even though he *saved my life?*"

"I'm grateful to him for saving your life—don't get

me wrong on that." Thomas leaned back in his chair—I could tell by that irritatingly smug look on his face that what I said no longer mattered. He'd already made up his mind on what he was going to do next. "But I'll only believe his story if he drinks truth potion brewed by a witch from the Haven and tells it to me himself."

19

RAVEN

THOMAS WAS ABOUT to send Noah in, and I had no idea what to say to him first. Because what Thomas had told me—about Noah being responsible for opening the Hell Gate—couldn't be true.

But why would he make something like that up? And Noah *was* super secretive…

Noah walked through the door, and the moment our eyes met, my doubts about him vanished. He looked at me with so much love that I knew as long as he was by my side, I'd be protected. Every bone in my body screamed at me to trust him.

Still, I needed to ask about what Thomas had said. Just to hear him deny it himself.

I also had to tell him all about Princess Ana. Because

that recording Thomas showed me of me pretending to be the vampire princess had seriously freaked me out.

But before I had a chance to do any of this, Noah shut the door behind him, pulled me into his arms, and kissed me. This kiss was more intense than the one when I'd first woken up, and it affirmed what that one had already showed me—that despite what Noah had told me back in New Orleans, my feelings for him were reciprocated.

My body filled with warmth as we kissed, and I wanted to pull him over to the couch and keep going.

I would have, if there wasn't so much we needed to discuss. But surprisingly, I wasn't the one who pulled away first—he was.

"Raven." Noah cupped my face with his hands, as if making sure I was really there and not just a figment of his imagination. "I lied to you back in New Orleans."

"I figured as much." I chuckled and leaned forward to kiss him again, but he stopped me. "What?" My stomach dropped—the look in his eyes was intense.

"We imprinted on each other," he said suddenly. "Back at that bar in New Orleans, when I kissed you for the first time."

"What?" I shook my head and leaned back, taking his hands in mine. I'd heard him, but what he'd just said... "That's impossible," I continued, although it didn't *feel* impossible—it felt right. It made sense, even though it also didn't. "You and Sage told me that shifters can only imprint on other shifters. Unless…"

"Unless what?" he asked.

"You're not saying I'm a shifter?" I asked. "Are you?"

"No." He laughed, amusement temporarily taking over the intensity in his gaze. "You're definitely not a shifter."

"Then what am I?" It was a question that had been eating at me for days. As far as I was aware, I was human. But then why were demons trying to abduct me? It didn't make any sense.

"You're human," he said. "Shifters have the best sense of smell of any supernatural. If you were something other than human, I'd smell it."

"So how did we imprint on each other?"

"I have no idea," he said. "This has never happened before."

"Great." I huffed and rolled my eyes, attempting to make light of the situation. "Not only are demons hunting me for unknown reasons, but I'm also the first human to ever imprint on a shifter. Just when I think things can't get any crazier, they do."

"Technically, I think *I* imprinted on *you*," he said. "And something about you allowed you to reciprocate. But yeah, pretty much."

He pulled me to him again, and we kissed for a few more blissful seconds. But as much as I wanted to do nothing but kiss Noah and forget about everything going on around us, I had questions. A *lot* of them.

I'd start with the ones that had to do with the imprint.

"Why did you lie to me back in New Orleans?" I stared up at him, my arms still wrapped around his neck. "Why pretend the imprinting didn't happen?"

He paused for a moment, his jaw clenched. "You know about the imprinting and mating process, right?" he asked, his eyes searching mine. "Sage told you?"

"She did." I nodded, thinking about the first one-on-one conversation I'd ever had with Sage, back in her plush, pink room in the Montgomery compound. It hadn't been long since then, but it felt like forever ago. "Shifters can imprint on multiple people, but they eventually choose one to mate with. Once they mate, that bond lasts forever."

"It never goes away." His eyes gleamed with intensity. "Even after death."

"Okay." I glanced down and shifted uncomfortably. "What does this have to do with you not telling me we imprinted on each other until now?"

"Because imprinting and mating is a curse as much as it's a gift," he said sharply. "Shifters either choose a mate, or never find true love. And that mating bond lasts for *life*. Once one mate dies, the other will never find love again. That's the way it's always been for us. But for you it's different. If you fall in love with someone and he dies, you'll eventually move on and fall in love again. But not if that person is me."

"Aren't you getting a bit ahead of yourself?" I asked, forcing a small smile. "We're young. We have the rest of our lives left to live."

"We're in a time of war," he reminded me. "Or did you already forget how close I came to dying the other day? How close *you* came to dying?"

I lowered my eyes and shook my head, since no, obviously I hadn't forgotten.

I just didn't want to think about it. I didn't want to live life terrified that each moment might be my last.

"I'm going to Avalon to *fight* in this war—to defeat the demons," he continued. "There's no saying what will happen to me. I'm a skilled fighter, but I'm not indestructible. If we let this progress between us, and if we become mates, I could be cursing you to a life without love. I don't want to do that to you. I *won't* do that to you."

His words felt like knives in my heart, and I focused on breathing steadily to calm the emotions raging through my body. It didn't work. "So... you don't want to give us a chance?" My voice shook—from either pain or anger. Maybe both. "You don't want to see where this connection between us can go?"

"It's not that I don't want to." He pinched his forehead together and breathed out in frustration. "I want to more than you could ever imagine." He dropped his hand back down, his eyes hardening. "But I can't. If anything happens to me, I want you to be happy, Raven. That won't happen if we become mates."

"If you truly believe that, why tell me at all?" I backed away from him, anger running through my veins like fire. "Why not keep lying to me, like you did in New Orleans?"

"That's what I wanted to do." He closed the distance between us and took my hands in his, squeezing them tightly and not letting them go. "But you nearly died in that alley back in Nashville. For a while I *thought* you were going to die. Thinking that you were going to die without knowing about our imprint, about how much I care about you—well, it just about killed me inside. I had to tell you. Even though we can't take this any farther, I needed you to know."

I was silent for a few seconds as I took it all in—and it was a *lot* to take in.

Maybe to him it sounded noble. But to me, it just sounded selfish.

"What about what I want?" I glared up at him, determined not to back down. "You keep talking about what you want and what would make *you* feel best. What if I don't agree? What if I want to give us a chance, no matter what might happen if we do?"

"That's just the imprint bond talking." He let go of my hands, and the space between us literally *hurt*. "Once it goes away, you'll start thinking clearly again."

"How can it just 'go away?'" I couldn't believe he was saying all of this. "Our souls are connected. I can *feel* it. I can feel your pain, your frustration, and your worry as intensely as if it were my own. That isn't the kind of thing that just 'goes away.'"

"It actually is," he said. "The imprint bond will disappear if I either mate with someone else or die."

Emptiness hit my chest at his words. "*Both* of those situations would devastate me," I said. Obviously death would be the worst, but if he imprinted on someone else... I couldn't bear to think about how badly that would hurt.

"You'd get over it." He spoke with such callousness that it shook me to the core.

"No." I shook my head slowly. "I don't think I would. The imprint bond is intense—I've never felt anything like it before. I don't think any human connection could ever compare."

"For your sake, I hope it can," he said.

Was this some kind of cruel joke? He was so determined to throw the imprint between us away—so determined to not give us a chance.

But I didn't have to sit back and accept it. I'd manifested my desires onto him before, and it had worked. Now, my desire to convince him to give us a chance was stronger than ever. Maybe I could manifest him into seeing things the way I did. It couldn't hurt to try.

And so, I reached for one of his hands and focused on the connection between us. *Give us a chance*, I thought, sending my desire his way. *See what might develop between us if we let it.*

He dropped his hand so quickly that you'd have thought my touch was burning him. "Stop that," he said.

"Stop what?" I smiled innocently, since there was no way he could know what I was trying to do.

"You're tapping into the imprint bond to try influencing me," he said. "I don't know how you knew to do that—only shifters know about the power of the imprint and mate bonds—but stop."

"I *didn't* know how to do it," I said. "I was just practicing manifestation."

"Manifestation?" He said it like he'd never heard the word before.

"Just something my mom taught me." I shrugged.

"The ability to will your wishes and desires to become reality. I'd always thought it was silly. But then I tried using it back when the rougarou captured us, and it worked. So I've been using it since."

He stared at me for a few seconds, as if waiting for me to add in a punch line. Then he laughed.

"What?" I crossed my arms and glared at him.

"Manifestation doesn't exist," he said once he got ahold of himself. "But when imprinted shifters are near each other, they can send emotions and desires to each other if they focus on it. I did it to you back in the alley. When I told you to run."

"I remember," I said. "I can't believe you thought I'd leave you there."

"Tapping into the imprint bond is more than just communicating what you want," he said. "The imprint bond connects our souls. When you tap into the imprint bond, you're literally nudging my soul to want what yours wants. To feel what you feel."

"Are you sure?" I asked. "Because even though I knew you wanted me to run from that alley, there wasn't a single second that I actually wanted to do it."

"I'm sure," he said. "But you've always been stubborn. I'm not surprised you resisted."

"It's a good thing I did," I said.

"It is," he agreed, which shocked me, since Noah

rarely admitted he was wrong. He was sort of like me that way. "But unless it's an emergency, don't use the imprint bond to influence my decisions. It's not respectful."

"Fine," I said, even though I felt far from it. "I'll just pretend the imprint bond doesn't exist." I stepped away from him, as if that would be enough to make the connection between us disappear. "That's what you want, right? For us to never have imprinted on each other at all?"

"Don't turn this into something it's not," he said. "All I want is to not hurt you. I just wish you could believe me and trust that I want what's best for you."

"After what Thomas told me earlier, I probably shouldn't trust you at all," I muttered.

Alarm flashed in Noah's eyes—he was so panicked that he looked like he stopped breathing for a second. "What did he tell you?" he asked.

"A lot of things." I leveled my gaze with his, glad that *I* was back in control of this conversation. "Mainly that you're also known as the First Prophet of the Vale, and that I'm also known as Princess Ana, a vampire from the Seventh Kingdom."

RAVEN

THE GUILT in Noah's eyes showed me I was right. He *was* the "First Prophet" Thomas had told me about.

I stood there silently, waiting for him to explain. Luckily, he didn't make a move for the door. If he did, I'd attempt to use my temporary vampire strength to stop him. Not that I thought that would work, since Noah was a trained fighter and all, but I'd definitely try.

"I don't know what you're talking about with Princess Ana," he said slowly. "But I can explain about my past as the First Prophet of the Vale."

"Really?" I raised an eyebrow. "Because Thomas said that the First Prophet—*you*—helped open the Hell Gate."

"And what did you say when Thomas told you that?" he asked.

"I told him he was wrong!" I threw out my arms, amazed he even had to ask. "I told him you'd never want to release demons from Hell. But now that you've confirmed you're the First Prophet, I don't know what to believe anymore."

"You should believe me," he said. "I'll tell you everything, right here right now. I didn't want to at first, because I didn't want you to be scared of me. But I'm done hiding things from you, Raven. You deserve to know the truth."

"Yeah," I agreed. "I do."

"It's a long story," he said. "We should probably sit down for it."

"All right." I plopped down onto the couch and watched as Noah did the same.

He sat close enough that we were nearly touching. I wanted to reach over and take his hand in mine so badly, but I resisted. It took strength—his body and soul called to me like a magnet—but I fought the pull.

Instead, I clasped my hands over my knees, watching him steadily, and said, "Tell me everything."

Noah *did* tell me everything—from the first dream he'd received from the demon who had claimed to be the wolves' Savior, to when the Earth Angel had ordered him to bring her back the teeth of ten demons he killed to prove he was worthy of entering Avalon. The story was long and twisted, and I hung onto every word with limited interruptions.

"Now you know all of it," he said once he was done. "I messed up. Big time."

"Yeah." I nodded. "You did."

"I'm doing everything I can to make up for it," he said. "So I hope you can find it in your heart to accept me anyway."

"I already have," I said honestly.

"Just like that?" He looked genuinely surprised.

"We're *imprinted* on each other." I took his hand, needing him to understand how important our connection was to me. "You're a good person—I knew that both before and after learning about your past. I know it because I can feel your soul. *You're* the one who refuses to accept *me*."

"I accept you," he said. "And I also accept that I'm not the best choice for you."

"I think I deserve a say in that decision."

He sighed and looked down at our joined hands, like he was struggling to decide if he should keep holding on or let go. He held on—for now. "I already explained my decision," he said. "I don't want to go through it again."

"Neither do I," I said, since all of this drama between us was emotionally exhausting. I wanted to convince him to give me a chance.

But when it came down to it, I couldn't *force* Noah to want to be with me.

If this was going to work between us, he was going to have to come to the decision to give us a chance on his own. We were both heading to the same place—Avalon—and the imprint bond between us was strong. We had time to let our relationship build. I was doing everything I could to allow that to happen.

But if he continued being so stubborn about trying to push me away, that wasn't the kind of relationship that would work for me long term, anyway. Being treated like that would make me miserable. It killed me to think it, because the imprint bond made me want to do everything possible to make things work between us, but it was true.

"Anyway, now you know about my history as the First Prophet," he said. "So what did you mean about you being Princess Ana?"

He was changing the subject on purpose. But I *did* want to ask him about Princess Ana, so I went along with it.

"Thomas showed me a recording of Princess Ana when she arrived to the Vale to enter the Bachelor-like competition Prince Jacen had for a wife." I motioned to the television, which was now off. "She was me."

"What are you talking about?" Noah scratched his head, looking genuinely confused.

"Princess Ana looked just like me," I said. "We're identical. And she was in the Vale when I was supposedly in Europe. So I think whoever took my memories had me pretend to be Princess Ana. They must have given me vampire blood—like Thomas just did—to give me the powers of a vampire princess. Then, once Prince Jacen eliminated me from the competition, they erased my memories and sent me back home. It would explain how I subconsciously knew what vampire blood can do for humans."

"It's not a bad theory," Noah said. "But it's not possible."

"You didn't see the recordings." I reached for the remote Thomas had used, but there were no buttons on it—not even an on switch. What kind of advanced technology *was* this? "Once Thomas is back, I'll have him show you. Princess Ana was me. I know it sounds crazy, but you'll believe it when you see it."

"That's not what I mean," he said. "I mean it's impossible because I know who Princess Ana was. She wasn't you."

"All right." I crossed one leg over the other, willing to humor him. "Then who was she?"

He looked me dead-on and said, "She was Annika."

RAVEN

I SAT UP IN SURPRISE. "The Earth Angel?" I asked.

"The one and only," he said. "Before becoming the Earth Angel, Annika was a human blood slave in the Vale. She worked with a witch named Geneva to infiltrate the palace. Geneva helped Annika disguise herself as a vampire princess and enter the competition to win Jacen's hand in marriage. Annika drank vampire blood to have the powers of a vampire princess, and transformation potion to change her appearance."

"To make herself look like *me*." I was breathless as the pieces started fitting together even more—and startled as a shattering realization fell into my lap. "But you were still in the Vale then. You've known I looked like Princess Ana this entire time."

I didn't want to believe he'd kept something so huge

from me. But after learning all of this, it was the only thing that made sense.

"I never met Annika when she was pretending to be Princess Ana," he explained, and I breathed slightly easier at the confirmation that my instincts about him weren't totally off. "In the Vale, the wolves lived outside of the vampire city. We didn't see anything that happened in there. I first saw Annika during the war at the Vale. By then, she was back in her true form. Trust me—if I'd known Princess Ana looked like you, I wouldn't have kept it from you. I swear it."

"Thank God." I held his gaze, my voice strong. "I was beginning to worry I was wrong in trusting you."

"You can trust me," he promised. "I'm on your side, Raven. Always."

There were so many unspoken words between us— so many intense emotions. His hand still held mine, and at that point, his touch was the only thing keeping me grounded as the world as I knew it crumbled around me.

A part of me wanted to kiss him again and make this entire mess go away—if only for a little while. And despite everything he'd said earlier about not wanting to see where this went between us, I could tell from the way he was looking at me that he wanted to kiss me, too. I could literally *feel* his desire through the imprint bond and hear our hearts beating in time together.

I leaned closer, and he did the same. It was like we were drawn together, and when his lips finally brushed mine, my heart leaped. I wanted to climb into his lap and melt right into him. Everything about him called to me—his taste, his scent, his touch. With my temporarily heightened vampire senses, it was more tempting than ever to let go and lose myself in the moment—and to him—completely.

But I pulled away, not allowing the kiss to progress any further.

In the span of a single second, he looked hurt, confused, and finally, resolved. "I'm sorry," he said. "I shouldn't have done that."

"Don't apologize." The last thing I needed was another reminder about his decision not to be with me. "We're just so close to figuring out the connection between Princess Ana and my missing memories," I said in a rush. "And as much as I want to just kiss you and make this all go away, it doesn't work like that."

He smiled mischievously and traced his thumb along my palm, sending warm tingles shooting through my body. "Are you so sure about that?" he teased.

"Yes." I couldn't help myself—I laughed. This playful

side of Noah was one I rarely saw, and I wanted to keep this version of him with me always.

Was this what he'd be like if he wasn't constantly carrying the weight of the world on his shoulders?

"All right, then." He pushed a few strands of hair off his forehead that must have fallen there when we'd kissed. "But after distracting me like that, you're going to have to remind me where we left off."

"Annika taking transformation potion to disguise herself while she was pretending to be Princess Ana." The seriousness of that implication suddenly set in—thanks to the lessons Noah and Sage had given me during our drives—and I immediately snapped back into focus. "Since Princess Ana looked like me, the transformation potion Annika was drinking was brewed with my blood. But transformation potions have to be used within twenty-four hours of being brewed, or they won't work..."

"And Annika was in the palace, disguised as Princess Ana, for over a week." The playfulness that had been in Noah's eyes a few seconds earlier was instantly replaced by horror. "Geneva would have needed daily access to your blood to keep up Annika's charade."

That name—Geneva—sounded so familiar. She was like a fuzzy image that refused to come into focus. But as hard as I tried to remember what she looked like, it was like trying to recall a forgotten dream.

A dream. *That's* how I knew her. I'd seen her in a cell, and my hands were wrapped around the bars…

"She locked me up somewhere," I realized. "Some kind of jail."

"How do you know that?" His grip on my hand tightened, his eyes wide with hope. "Do you remember?"

"Not really." I lowered my eyes, knowing it wasn't the answer he wanted to hear. "I think I might be having dreams about what happened when my memories were erased. But when I wake up, I can barely remember them. All that's left is a flash—a feeling. But the name Geneva is familiar. And in the dreams, I'm pretty sure I was trapped somewhere. I was holding onto bars that looked like they were part of a jail cell. But that's all I can remember." I shrugged, wishing I could give him more.

"As much as I hate it, it makes sense." Noah's eyes blazed at my mention of being kept in a cell. "Geneva needed your blood each day to brew Annika's transformation potion, so she would have had to keep you somewhere. Probably the same place she was keeping the royal vampire whose blood she was giving to Annika. In separate cells, obviously. To make sure you stayed alive."

Even though it hadn't happened, I shivered at the thought of a vampire draining me dry. "Why do you think she was keeping that vampire prisoner?" I asked.

"How else would she have gotten his or her blood?" he asked in return.

"Thomas thinks the vampire royal who was giving Annika blood was in on the plan," I said. "Not just in on it—he thinks that vampire *devised* the plan to spy on the Vale."

"Thomas is wrong," Noah said. "The plan was Annika's. Geneva was working for her."

"Are you sure?" I asked, although I could tell by the confident way he'd said it that he was.

"Yes."

"Good." I ran my fingers through my hair, amazed by how perfectly this was falling into place. "Because if Geneva was creating transformation potion with my blood, I'd bet she was the witch who gave me the memory potion, too. Which means she can create an antidote, and I can get my memories back."

"No," he said. "She can't."

"Why not?" I frowned.

"Because Geneva's dead."

RAVEN

"WHAT?" Everything was coming together so nicely, and then he had to drop *that* bomb on me.

"After the Hell Gate was opened, Geneva sacrificed herself to close it," he continued. "Of course, that didn't put all the escaped demons back inside, but it stopped more of them from getting out. If she hadn't sacrificed herself, the demons would have had the numbers to take over the Earth immediately. We wouldn't have stood a chance."

I took a few moments to let his words sink in. "Well, then I'm grateful for her sacrifice," I said slowly, meaning it. Because of her, everyone on Earth had a fighting chance. That was worth more than anything. "But with Geneva dead, I'll never be able to get my memories back. Right?"

"We don't know for sure that she's the one who erased your memories," he said. "But she was the strongest witch in the world. If anyone could have created a potion capable of erasing *weeks* worth of memories, it would have been her."

I bit my lip and nodded. If we were right—which it seemed like we were—it made sense that Geneva had created the memory potion. And the only witch who could create the antidote was the witch who had created the potion.

Which meant I'd never get my memories back.

"What are you thinking?" Noah asked. Our hands were still clasped together, and neither of us was making any move to pull away.

"I'm thinking that I should be okay with the fact that I might never get my memories back," I said. "I mean, it seems like Geneva locked me in a jail cell. And while I don't remember what happened there, in my dreams I'm always terrified. Maybe it's a good thing I don't remember."

"Maybe." Noah didn't look convinced.

"But I'm *not* okay with not remembering," I continued, allowing the anger I felt to seep into my tone. "I don't think I ever will be. Those weeks were just erased. Whatever happened to me—no matter how awful it was

—I want to know. And I hate that it might always be blank."

"I understand," Noah said, and from the way he was looking at me, I could tell he did. He could probably feel what I was feeling through the imprint bond. "When we get to Avalon, maybe Annika will be able to help fill in the blanks for you."

I shifted uncomfortably, knowing he wasn't going to like what I had to say next. But I needed to ask. "Are you sure Annika's trustworthy?" I asked.

"She's the Earth Angel." He looked at me like I'd gone nuts. "She was shown the way to Avalon by the angels in Heaven themselves. She's raising an army of Nephilim to defeat the demons—to stop them from killing all supernaturals and taking the Earth for themselves. The fate of both supernatural and humankind is on her. She's the one person in this world we can trust more than anyone."

"But she had Geneva imprison me for my blood, and she walked around looking like me for days." I shuddered, not liking the thought of someone using my body as a disguise. It wasn't actually me—it was just an illusion that made her look like me—but it was still weird. "If she's as good and trustworthy as you say, why would she do that to me?"

"I don't know," Noah admitted. "It doesn't match up

with what I know about her. But she *has* to have a reason. I'm not going to pretend I know what that reason is, because I don't. But once we get to Avalon, you'll be able to ask her yourself."

"I know," I said, since as much as I hated it, he was right. With Geneva dead, Annika was the best person to help me fill in the blanks from where my memories had been erased.

But that didn't mean I'd ever be okay with what she did.

"Plus, Rosella told you that you have to go to Avalon to save your mom," Noah added. "So you better not be backing out of it now."

"Oh, I'm still going to Avalon," I said. "I didn't come this far—and risk my life multiple times—for nothing."

"Good." He smiled. "Just wanted to make sure."

Electricity buzzed between us, and I desperately wanted to kiss him again. But before I could, the door to the media room swung open.

Noah was instantly at his feet in front of me with his slicer in hand, ready to fight to protect me.

But he didn't need to. Because Thomas marched inside, holding a vial of light blue potion in his hand—truth potion. Sage followed behind him.

I stood as well, not wanting to be the only one sitting down.

"I just had an interesting conversation with Sage about your history as the First Prophet of the Vale." Thomas glanced at Noah's slicer like it was an annoyance that didn't belong in the room. "Put your weapon away. There's no need for such hostility between us— not after I just saved your girlfriend's life."

Noah put the slicer back in his weapons belt, although he remained on guard.

"I take it you've had time to fill Raven in on everything you kept from her?" Thomas asked. "Because she was mighty clueless when I spoke with her earlier."

"Yes." Noah glared at Thomas as he spoke. "She knows everything now."

"Good," Thomas said. "Because I have important information to give you, as I want to work *with* you and not against you. But first, you're going to have to prove you're trustworthy." He held up the potion, making it clear what he meant. "Can you do that?"

"I already went through all this with Flint." Noah sounded annoyed more than anything. "Sage was there. Ask her."

"She told me." Thomas didn't look moved in the slightest. "But this truth potion is stronger than the one Flint gave you. It was brewed by one of the witches of the Haven. Taking it shouldn't be a problem... unless there's something you're trying to hide?"

I looked over at Noah and nodded. As long as he was being honest with us all—which I believed he was—there was no reason for him not to drink the potion.

"I'm not hiding anything." Noah held his hand out, and Thomas passed the truth potion over to him.

"Fantastic." Thomas eyed Noah up, as if he expected Noah to try breaking out of the room at any second. "Well, then. Cheers."

"Cheers." Noah opened the cap, held the vial up in a toast, and then downed the light blue liquid all in one gulp.

23

SAGE

THE FOUR OF us situated ourselves on the couch—Noah and Raven sat close together, and I made sure to put as much distance between Thomas and myself as I could.

Just like I knew he would, Noah told Thomas the same story of his past as the First Prophet of the Vale that he'd told me. I understood why Thomas was being cautious by making Noah tell his story under truth potion again, and I was also relieved to learn that my trust in Noah hadn't been misplaced.

"Anything else you want to know?" Noah asked Thomas once he finished.

"No," Thomas said, a satisfied smile on his face. "I think we're good here."

"Great." I wished more than anything that I could reduce the tension between the two guys. So I turned to

Thomas and asked, "What's this important information you have for us?"

I hoped it was information about whoever had sent the coyotes after us on our way to New Orleans. They hadn't tried attacking again, but I knew better than to think that meant we were safe.

"It's about your brother." Thomas faced me, watching me with what looked like pity. "You're not going to like it."

"What sort of trouble has Flint gotten himself into this time?" I sighed and rolled my eyes. I hadn't expected this to be about Flint, but I wasn't surprised. Flint was the alpha of one of the most powerful shifter packs in the country. You didn't get to his level by being the nice guy all the time.

You got there by making people respect and fear you. And Flint could be a pretty scary guy.

He'd also do anything to protect our pack. So I trusted that no matter what Thomas was about to say, Flint would have his reasons for doing it.

But something about the way Thomas was looking at me made me brace myself for the worst.

"Before the three of you showed up at my doorstep, Flint called me," Thomas started. "He told me you'd be arriving soon."

"He couldn't have." I scrunched my eyebrows

together, confused. "I never told him we were coming here. He hasn't known where we've been since New Orleans."

"Nonetheless, he knew you were coming," he continued. "He told me you were with the First Prophet, and that the First Prophet had brainwashed you."

"I don't understand." I looked back and forth between Noah and Thomas, feeling like I was in a daze. "That doesn't make any sense."

"Not according to Flint," Thomas said, and he proceeded to tell us about the entire phone conversation he'd had with my brother.

Flint had asked Thomas to bring me back to LA. He'd said he was working on an alliance and that he needed me there to cement it.

Flint had said Noah had lied about his quest to kill the demons. That he'd stolen the assignment from someone else.

"That's why you wanted Noah to take truth potion and confirm his story," I realized. "You were checking to see if Flint was lying or not."

"Precisely," Thomas said. "Especially since Flint asked me to kill Noah and Raven."

I sat forward, instantly on guard. "What?" I widened my eyes, not willing to believe it.

"Obviously, I have no intention of harming either of

them." Thomas motioned in Noah and Raven's direction, as if proving they were unharmed. "Although if Noah's story hadn't checked out, the situation would have been different, of course. So it's a good thing wolf boy here was telling the truth."

"Flint wouldn't..." I trailed off, shaking my head in disbelief.

"He would," Thomas said. "And he did. As you know, I record all of my conversations. You're free to listen if you need proof."

"Please." I wouldn't believe it—at least not until I heard it myself. Even then, Thomas could always fake it. But I knew my brother.

If it was really my brother speaking on that phone call, I'd know.

"I figured as much." Thomas removed the latest iPhone from his pocket, and the conversation between him and Flint started to play.

I sat there in horror as I listened. It went exactly how Thomas had claimed.

Once it ended, the four of us sat there in silence.

"Flint knew about the coyotes." Raven, surprisingly enough, was the one to break the silence. "Was he the one who sent them after us?"

"It would explain why the coyotes wanted to take Sage somewhere with them," Noah said. "And why they wanted us dead. If they'd gotten away with it, they were probably going to bring Sage back to LA. Just like Flint asked Thomas to do."

My head buzzed, all of the information spinning so much that it felt like my brain was about to implode. I heard the others talking around me, but I couldn't focus on what they were saying.

Why would my brother do this? What kind of alliance was he making? Why hadn't he just *told* me about it?

If he'd talked to me, I would have listened. I probably would have gone back to LA on my own. I wouldn't have liked abandoning Noah on his hunt—and I would have returned to helping him once the alliance was solidified—but pack came first. Always.

From the easy way they accepted this, Thomas, Noah, and Raven apparently had no problems villainizing my brother. But I couldn't just sit here and listen to this. I needed to call Flint and set things right with him myself.

I took my phone out of my bag, pressed the button to call him, and held the phone to my ear.

It didn't ring. Instead, it beeped three times and the call ended automatically.

I took a look at the screen—no service.

"Not getting through?" Thomas smirked and eyed up

my phone.

"You're blocking my service," I realized. "Lift it and let me call him. I have a right to talk to my brother."

"How's that possible?" Raven looked back and forth between Thomas and me in confusion, finally settling her gaze on Thomas. "How can you block Sage's cell service?"

24

RAVEN

"WHAT DO you know about gifted vampires?" Thomas answered my question with one of his own.

Vampires had been one of the first topics covered in my long car rides with Sage and Noah, so I sat proudly, glad that I knew what he was talking about. "When some vampires are turned, human attributes of theirs can be strengthened," I said. "For instance, as a human, Rosella was able to see the future. That ability was heightened when she was turned. It's why she's a seer as a vampire."

"Who told you that?" he asked.

"Noah and Sage," I said.

"They were close, but not exactly right," he said. "I lived in the Haven for a while after being turned, so I'm friends with Rosella. As a human, she was talented at listening to people, observing them, and using that information to determine what choices they might make. She had the gift of intuition. Once she was turned into a vampire, that ability heightened, allowing her to actually see the future."

"All right." I nodded, glad I'd seen Rosella's gift in action with my own eyes. Otherwise, I might not have believed him. "I'm going to go out on a limb here and guess you're bringing this up because you also have a gift?"

"Yes," he said. "As a human, I had a knack for technology. With a bit of fiddling, I could quickly determine how any gadget worked and fix anything that was broken. As a vampire..." He paused, giving me a close-lipped smile. "Well, it's probably best to simply show you."

Suddenly, all of the cell phones in the room started buzzing and lighting up. It was like they'd taken on lives of their own. The lights started flickering—like in those creepy horror movies. And it wasn't just the phones. The television turned on and began flipping through the channels. The lights overhead went crazy as well.

Thomas looked completely in his element as the eerie, flickering lights bounced off his skin. I watched him, shocked. Then, all at once, everything returned to normal.

"You did that," I stated, knowing it was true.

"I can communicate with and control technology." He was so casual about it—as if what he was saying was normal. "I'm what's known as a technopath."

"That's why your remote control doesn't have a power button." I glanced at where the strange, blank remote sat. "You didn't need to use it at all."

"It's a prop—I only held it to keep you focused and not asking more questions," he said. "And earlier, you asked how I had recordings from Prince Jacen's selection in the Vale. The answer is simple—I hacked in and created recordings for myself. I thought they might prove useful down the line." He smiled, clearly proud of himself for being right.

This guy would be a nightmare to security systems everywhere. No wonder he kept referring to his penthouse as a fortress. I had a feeling that I'd only seen a sliver of all the advanced technology he had here. He'd likely used his ability to acquire his wealth, too.

"That's... amazing," I finally said, not wanting him to see how his power was making me feel slightly uncomfortable. "It's a good thing we have you on our side, isn't it?"

"It is." He nodded. "I can be a pretty terrifying enemy. None of the vampire kingdoms want any trouble with the Bettencourt coven. Most vampires in

America have to go rogue to avoid detection by the kingdoms, but not us. As long as we don't make the humans suspicious about what we are, the kingdoms let us be."

"How do you get enough blood for yourself and your coven without drawing attention to yourselves?" It was something I'd been wondering since I woke up here and learned that the Bettencourt coven was smack in the middle of one of the biggest cities in America.

"There are microscopic security cameras in every hotel room—"

"Isn't that against the law?" I interrupted.

"Against human law." He chuckled. "I have ways around that. But did you want the answer to your question or not?"

"Sorry," I said. "Go on."

"We prefer to target humans who are traveling alone —it's easier that way," he said. "But most importantly, we always make sure they're strong and healthy. Because once they're asleep, we go into their room and draw their blood. We take the same amount as is safe to give for a blood donation. The blood is stored in our refrigerated vault. Once done, the human is given memory potion to forget what happened, and healing potion so there's no trace of the needle mark. The next day, they'll feel woozy, but they won't know what happened. And we never take blood from a human more than once during their stay."

"Wow." I shook my head, unsure what to make of this. "Don't any of them realize something's off?" I was mainly thinking about the way I knew my memories of my Europe trip weren't *right*. Surely some of the humans who'd gone through this process had experienced the same thing?

"There are a few rumors of hauntings in the hotel—those silly city ghost tours love stopping outside as part of their presentations—but the humans are clueless about what truly goes on here," he said. "And I keep my vampires in line. Only those who have proven their ability to resist draining a bleeding human are allowed to perform the extractions. In all of the decades we've owned and lived in this hotel, we've only had one mistake."

"You mean a death," I said darkly.

"A death that was our fault," he corrected me. "Occasionally, humans will die of natural causes while staying here—it happens in any hotel. In those cases, we go through the human system to report the death and take care of the body. But in regards to the human death that was our fault, that vampire was punished most severely. There have been no transgressions since. We keep our guests safe. I promise you that."

"But you go into their hotel rooms while they're sleeping and take their blood." Goosebumps rose on my arms at the thought.

"And then they forget it ever happened and continue their lives as normal," he said. "It's far more humane than what happens in the kingdoms."

"What happens in the kingdoms?" I leaned forward, not sure I wanted to hear the answer. Sage and Noah hadn't given me the details there. All I knew was that other than the Haven, the vampires in the kingdoms fed on human blood.

"That's a conversation for another day." Thomas waved my question and zeroed in on Sage, who had a glazed look in her eyes. "Right now, we need to decide what to do about Flint."

25

SAGE

"You're crazy if you think I'm going to turn against my brother so easily." I glared at Thomas and sat straighter. He'd shattered my heart, and now he wanted me to side with him over Flint? Over my *pack*?

"You heard what he said." Thomas motioned to his phone.

The evidence looked bad, but I wouldn't be swayed that easily. "You could have used your ability to manipulate that recording into something it wasn't," I said.

"Why would I do that?" he asked.

"I don't know," I replied. "But I know you well enough to know you always have a motive. Even if I don't know what that motive is yet."

His eyes clouded with darkness—like my words had hurt him. "I'm trying to protect you," he said.

"Then help us find out who really sent those coyotes after us." My voice rose—I couldn't believe he was still pushing this. "Because it wasn't Flint. My brother wouldn't do that."

"I disagree, but I'm not the only one who's met Flint before." Thomas looked over at Noah. "You've been pretty quiet this whole time. What do you think about all this?"

Noah pressed his lips together and looked back and forth between Thomas and me, like he couldn't choose between us.

What was taking him so long to reply? Flint had allowed Noah to live in our pool house when he would have otherwise been homeless. Noah should have stood up for Flint on the spot.

"These are serious allegations." Noah pressed the pads of his fingers together, being careful about his wording, and looked at Thomas. "While I don't know much about how your ability works, I trust Sage that you could have used it to alter—or create—the conversation you played for us."

I breathed out in relief. Noah was standing up for me —for my pack. Thank God.

"The conversation you heard wasn't altered," Thomas said. "It was a recording of what actually happened."

"Very well." Noah leaned back in the couch, a mischievous glint in his eyes. "Do you have more vials of the truth potion you had me take lying around here?"

"Yes." Thomas didn't flinch when he answered the question.

"Good," Noah said. "Take it, and *then* tell us the recording hasn't been altered in any way."

"You can't be serious." I glared at Noah. "You actually think he might be telling the truth?"

"We have to consider the possibility," Noah said. "Trust me—I don't like the thought of Flint putting a bounty on my and Raven's heads, and I hate that he could be plotting behind your back. But if that's what's going on, we need to know. We need to be prepared." He turned back to Thomas. "So—what do you say? Will you take the truth potion or not?"

"Your proposal is fair." Thomas nodded and stood up. "I'll go get the potion."

He returned less than a minute later with a vial of light blue potion. He untwisted the cap and raised it to his lips, preparing to drink it.

"Wait." Noah held a hand up, and Thomas stopped mid-motion. "Let me smell it, so I can make sure it's the same strength as the one you just gave me."

Smart. Shifters had the best noses of any supernatural species. Noah would easily be able to sniff the potion and tell if it was as strong as the one he'd just drank.

Thomas handed over the potion.

Noah held it under his nose and inhaled. "It's good." He nodded and handed it back to Thomas. "Go ahead."

Thomas downed the potion like it was a shot. Then he placed the empty vial next to where the one Noah had previously taken was sitting on the coffee table. "I hope you know that I'm telling you this because I want to keep you safe," he said, focused on me.

I swallowed, sweat beading on my forehead. This media room was feeling smaller by the second. I wanted to know the truth, but if the recording was real…

A pit formed in my stomach at the possibility. Because if the recording was real, I wouldn't be able to trust my brother or my pack.

I'd be alone.

I wasn't scared by much, but the thought of being alone terrified me.

"Do you want to ask, or should I?" Noah's voice interrupted my thoughts.

"I can do it." I straightened and turned to Thomas, not wanting him to see my fear. "Was the conversation you just played for us an accurate, unaltered recording of the discussion you had with Flint within the past few days?" I was careful to word my question properly, as I didn't want to give Thomas a way to lie by omission.

"Yes." Thomas held his gaze with mine. "Hours before you arrived to my penthouse, Flint called me. I recorded the conversation, and what you heard was an accurate, unaltered version of what we discussed. I know it's hard to hear, but I'm telling you this because I love you and I want to keep you safe no matter what."

The walls felt like they closed in around me. My chest ached—it hurt to breathe—and I pressed my fingers to my temples as I tried to sort through my thoughts. How could my brother do this—not just to me, but to Noah? Because Flint knew the truth about Noah. He knew Noah was fighting for a good cause.

I wasn't stupid—I knew my brother's morals tended to reside in a gray area. But he always had reasons for what he did. He made tough decisions to protect me. To protect our pack.

"This doesn't make sense." I lowered my hands and looked at Thomas again. I couldn't even think about how he'd said he loved me while under the influence of truth potion. I needed to take this one step at a time. "Why wouldn't Flint just call me, tell me about this alliance, and ask me to come home?"

"Because whatever this alliance is, he knows you're not going to like it," Thomas said.

"He told you that?" I asked.

"No," he said. "It's just a guess."

"But it makes sense," Noah added. "Especially since someone in this alliance apparently wants me dead. In case you forgot that part."

"No," I said numbly. "I didn't forget."

I looked at Raven, curious what she was thinking. She'd been pretty quiet this whole time, but now, I saw sadness in her eyes.

She didn't have to speak for me to understand what was going through her mind. She agreed with what the guys were saying. She felt bad for me. But worst of all, she understood how scared I was.

Because now, she wasn't the only one who might have lost her family.

"You have a place here," Thomas finally said. "You can move back into your old room—"

"Stop," I interrupted him. "I'm not moving in here."

Move in with my ex-fiancée in his hotel run by vampires? No, thanks.

"You don't have to take your old room back," he said. "You can have a condo of your own, if you'd prefer."

"No." I stared him down, my voice sharp. "I'm not just going to abandon my pack."

"You heard what Flint said," Thomas said. "You can't go back there."

"I can, and I will." I stood up and ran my fingers through my hair, needing to get out of this room. I turned to Noah and Raven, since they were the ones in danger here—not Thomas. "I'm going to figure out what my brother's up to and talk some sense into him. The only way to do that is to see him in person. But I need to make sure you're both safe first. So I'm going to wait until you've made your way to Avalon."

"Or you could come with us," Noah said. "To Avalon. It's the safest place in the world. Rumor has it that not even the fae can find it."

"The Bettencourt is just as safe," Thomas cut in. "More so, since you have me to protect you here."

"I don't need to be protected from my own brother!" I yelled, stunning them all into silence.

I wasn't sure who I was trying to convince more— them, or myself.

All three of them sat there with wide eyes, apparently not sure what to say next.

"I need some time to think." I marched toward the door, stopping when my hand was wrapped fully around the doorknob and turning to face them once more. "I'll be in my room. Don't come and talk to me unless it's to tell me that the vampire blood is out of Raven's system."

"Why?" Raven asked.

"Because once it is, we have a final demon to track down and kill," I said. "Then the two of you can go to Avalon, and I can go back home to talk to my brother."

26

SAGE

I'D HOPED to get a ton of sleep that night and wake up feeling refreshed and ready to face my problems the next day.

That didn't happen. Instead, I tossed and turned for hours, trying to think about who Flint might have made an alliance with.

One of the vampire kingdoms?

The fae?

The demons themselves?

Each idea was more ridiculous than the last, and all this worrying was getting me nowhere. I'd only know the truth once I went back home and found it out myself. For now, I was frustrated, irritated, and scared. I didn't know what to do with all of these emotions. All I knew was that I needed to be alone.

Much to my relief, the three of them listened to me and didn't come in to bother me. Thomas knew me well enough that he knew trying to push me would just make things worse.

He also knew me well enough to know that when I was upset and couldn't sleep, I liked to binge watch television shows. When I'd stomped back to my room, the television screen had flashed on, showing the Netflix home screen. My account was still there.

He'd used his power to let me know my account hadn't been deleted.

I wished I could say I was annoyed at him. But when I logged into my account and immediately found a show to watch, I was grateful.

Binge watching television didn't make me forget about everything going on, but it did distract me slightly. That was the best I could hope for right now. Especially given what Thomas had said to me under the truth potion.

He'd said he loved me.

I wished he'd never said it. Now I was more confused than ever, and given everything going on with my brother, confusion was the last thing I needed right now.

Anyway, truth potion only forced people to say what they *believed* to be true. If someone believed a lie to be true, they'd say that lie under truth potion, because it was *their* truth.

Thomas might have believed he loved me, but he didn't act like it. And weren't actions more important than anything else?

I thought so.

At some point, someone left a large pizza outside my door, covered in delicious meat toppings. I knew it was there because the smell was intoxicating. I opened the door, glad to see that no one was standing in the hall, and pulled the pizza inside.

This had to be thanks to either Thomas or Noah. Both of them were aware of my weakness for fast food delivery pizza. I didn't care how many times people swore by high-end pizza restaurants—nothing could ever be as delicious as Dominos. And when I was stressed, I could easily polish off an entire large by myself. Plus a side of cheese bread.

Once I was full, I finally managed to fall asleep.

A knock on the door woke me up what felt like mere minutes later.

I opened my eyes to see the "are you still watching this?" Netflix screen on the television, and the empty pizza box open at the end of the bed. Apparently I'd slept for a few hours, but it didn't feel like it. I felt like I could sleep for a full day straight.

I was the definition of a train wreck. But a glance at my watch told me I needed to get myself together, because the vampire blood was likely out of Raven's system by now.

"Sage?" Raven opened the door a crack and peered inside. She frowned when she saw me, and she opened the door slightly wider. "The vampire blood is out of my system."

"No blood hangover?" I asked.

"The witch who lives here gave me a potion to counteract it," she said. "The guys sent me to come get you…" She pointed her thumb behind her and trailed off. "What should I tell them?"

The concern on her face gave away what she was thinking—I didn't look ready to re-emerge. But I couldn't lounge in bed for days on end. I needed to get out and face my problems.

That started with getting myself together.

"I need to freshen up." I rolled out of bed, feeling huge and bloated after my massive pig out. Carbs never sat as well with me as pure protein, but they were so delicious that sometimes I couldn't resist. "Tell them I'll be out in a few minutes."

The break from all the craziness had been nice.

But now, it was time to get a grip on myself and face reality.

27

SAGE

I WALKED through the living room and saw my and Noah's suitcases sitting in the foyer. Thomas must have sent someone to Nashville to retrieve our stuff. That was great, since we had weapons and potions back there that I didn't feel like taking the time to reacquire.

Hopefully he'd also checked us out of the hotel. I'd have to call later and make sure.

For now, I heard voices coming from the dining room, so I headed in that direction.

Thomas, Noah, and Raven were all gathered around someone sitting at the head of the table. Raven moved aside and I saw that the person who'd joined us was Cassandra—one of the witches who lived in the Bettencourt. On the table in front of her was a cloth, an atlas opened to a map of the central United States, a pendulum, candles, and crystals. Her blonde hair was longer than I remembered, but other than that, she didn't look like she'd aged a day since the last time I'd seen her. We looked the same age now.

The moment her eyes met mine, she smiled and stood up. "Sage." She walked toward me and embraced me in a hug. "It's been too long."

"Four years." Well, *almost* four years. It would be exactly four years by the end of summer.

She pulled away and studied me, watching me with concern. I was sure she had a lot of questions for me. But Cassandra was the queen of proper manners, so she'd wait for a more appropriate time.

Meaning, a time when Thomas, Noah, and Raven *weren't* hovering over our shoulders listening to everything we said.

"While you were sleeping, Thomas and your two new friends caught me up on what's going on," she said.

My heart leaped into my chest, and I glanced at Noah in panic. "Everything?" I asked.

"We covered the basics," Noah said. "My quest from the Earth Angel, you getting on board, Raven joining our group, and our most recent hunt leading us here."

I nodded, understanding exactly what he'd left out. Mainly, every crazy, weird thing that had happened to us from Noah being the First Prophet, Raven's missing memories and her knowing about the power of vampire blood, to Flint making a super shady alliance behind my back.

"Cassandra agreed to scry for the location of the final demon," Thomas added.

"Great." I avoided Thomas's gaze and smiled at Cassandra. "Thank you."

I should have been excited—this was the last demon we'd scry for. Assuming Cassandra was able to locate a demon, we were getting closer than ever to finishing this hunt. Especially given how much quicker each kill had been with Raven on board, given that the demons were drawn to her like moths to a flame.

It also represented the end of an era. Sure, I'd only been on this hunt with Noah for a few weeks, but it felt like we'd known each other for so much longer. And while the hunt was dangerous, it was also exhilarating and fun. It gave me a *purpose* I didn't know I craved.

Once it was over, I'd have to go back home and face Flint. Then, once I leveled with him and helped him out of whatever bind he'd gotten himself into, everything would go back to normal.

I should have been glad. Relieved. Happy about the prospect of returning to my pack.

But I wasn't sure I wanted normal anymore. Especially given the state of the world right now. With the demons lying low, too many supernaturals were in denial that they could actually overpower us. They didn't think enough demons had escaped Hell to do the type of damage people were claiming they could.

Not me. I'd seen firsthand how dangerous the demons could be.

If we wanted to survive, we needed to step up, band together, and fight. I intended on being a part of that.

Cassandra walked back over to the head of the table. "Are you ready to begin?" she asked.

"Yes." I walked to the edge of the table and put my hands on the glass. "Let's do this."

28

SAGE

CASSANDRA SET the candles in their places—each one representing a point of the compass and an element of the Earth—and lit them. As each flame caught, I smelled the element the candle represented. Forest for earth, sea salt for water, flowers for air, and smoke for fire.

She reached for her pendulum and glanced at Noah. "I'll need the heavenly weapon you've been using to hunt the demons," she said.

Noah pulled the slicer out of his weapons belt and handed it over.

The moment the slicer was in Cassandra's hand, the pendulum started to move.

That was fast.

The only other time it had started moving *that*

quickly was when Amber had located the demon that had been a few miles away in LA.

Cassandra moved her hand to follow the swinging of the pendulum. Sure enough, the crystal ended up right above the dot labeled Chicago.

"Flip to the city's map," she instructed, since if she broke contact with either the pendulum or the slicer, the spell would be broken.

Raven reached for the atlas, flipped through it, and placed it back down once it was opened to a map of Chicago. The pendulum started swinging again. It eventually settled on a place a few blocks away—a street full of bars and clubs.

Of course. If there was one thing we'd learned on these hunts, it was that the demons were searching for people in crowded areas. It made popular bars and clubs the perfect places for them to prowl. We still weren't sure why the demons were choosing certain humans to kidnap, but given that Raven had been one of the humans selected, we hoped to figure out the answer soon.

Well, Noah and Raven hoped to figure out the answer once they reached Avalon.

I might never find out, since I'd be going back home.

Again, I wished this hunt wasn't so close to ending. There were too many questions still unanswered. A part of me—a bigger part than I cared to admit—yearned to go with Noah and Raven to Avalon. There, I could join the Earth Angel's army and continue doing my part to stop the demons from taking over the Earth.

But I had to figure out what was going on with my brother and help him out of whatever mess he'd created.

Pack first, always. Especially since Flint was a stickler to tradition, which meant if I joined the Earth Angel's army on Avalon, I'd be a deserter to the Montgomery pack. I'd never be welcomed back again.

The pack was my family. Leaving them would feel like ripping out part of my soul.

"Sage?" Noah pulled me out of my dark thoughts. "Are you ready to head out and kill our last demon?"

"Yeah." I shook the thoughts out of my mind and forced a smile. "I'm ready."

"Good." Thomas looked at Noah, then at Raven, and finally at me—that annoyingly gorgeous self-satisfied smirk on his lips the entire time. "So am I."

SAGE

"WHAT DO you have to be ready for?" I asked.

"The hunt." His eyes twinkled with amusement. "I'm coming with you."

"No." I shook my head adamantly. "You're not."

He held my gaze, not saying a word.

I stared right back. If this was how he was going to play it, so be it. I could hold my own in a standoff when I needed to.

"I'll leave the four of you to discuss how you plan to proceed." Cassandra blew out the candles and gathered her materials into the cloth she'd laid out on the table. "I'm glad to have helped, but I have some work I need to attend to in my apothecary. Hopefully I'll be seeing more of you soon." She flashed me a friendly smile and made her way out of the penthouse.

The moment she was gone, I turned my attention back to Thomas. "The three of us have this under control," I said. "We don't need help."

"Are you so sure about that?" he asked.

"Of course." I crossed my arms, annoyed at him for doubting my competency. "We've been doing this for a while."

"I know you have," he said. "But you told me yourselves that the last demon you hunted was stronger than the others—you suspected he was a warrior demon. He had a potion that prevented you from shifting. And he brought that red-eyed wolf with him. If Raven hadn't risked her life by using Noah's heavenly weapon, there's a good chance you would all be dead by now."

"We just have to be more careful this time around," I said. "We'll find a smaller alley to corner the demon in. We'll make sure no one's with him. Now that we know to look out for an accomplice, we can be more prepared."

"You'll be more prepared if I'm with you," Thomas said. "I'll be another set of eyes. Plus, that potion that prevented you from shifting won't do anything to me. What's the harm in my coming with you?"

I fidgeted with the cloaking ring around my finger, looking for a reason other than *you broke my heart and I don't want to be around you for any longer than necessary.*

"The demon will know what you are," I said. "You'd give us away before we had a chance to strike."

"Come on, Sage." He shook his head in disappointment. "I don't normally wear it because I have no need to hide what I am, but do you really think I don't have a cloaking ring of my own?"

"I've never seen you wear one." I shrugged.

"I have one," he said. "And I'm happy to wear it if it means I can accompany you on your mission."

"It's not a bad plan," Raven chimed in. I glared at her, but she continued anyway. "I mean, we definitely could have used his help last time. And we still don't know what that red-eyed shifter was. For all we know, the demon tonight could also have one with him—or more than one. We'll be more prepared if Thomas comes with us."

"So the vote's one to one." Thomas turned to Noah. "Looks like the decision is up to you."

Noah looked back and forth between Raven and me. From the apology in his eyes when he looked at me, I knew what he was going to say before he said it.

"I agree with Raven," he said, confirming my suspicion. "Given the possibility of another—or more than one—red-eyed shifter, and the fact that the last demon we fought had that potion that stopped me from shifting, it'll be beneficial to have a vampire on our side.

Especially a prince with a gift for controlling technology."

"You're smarter than I initially gave you credit for," Thomas said to him.

"Not so fast." Noah gave Thomas a stone cold glare that shut him up immediately. "Sage has been hunting with me since nearly the beginning. I wouldn't have gotten this far without her help. So unless you can get her on board, the three of us are going on this hunt alone."

Thomas nodded in respect. "Understood," he said. "Would you mind giving Sage and me some time alone?"

"Five minutes," Noah said. "We've already pinpointed the demon's location, so we can't afford to lose any more time than that."

"Five minutes," Thomas agreed.

Noah reached for Raven's hand, and the two of them exited the dining room.

The moment they were gone, the doors slid closed, leaving Thomas and me alone.

I faced him with fire in my eyes. "What are you going to do?" I asked. "Keep me locked in here until I agree to let you come with us?"

"I wouldn't keep you anywhere against your will," he said. "You should know me better than that."

"I used to know you." I huffed. "Not anymore."

"You know me well enough to trust that I'd help Raven, even though you had information that any other vampire would have killed you for knowing," he said.

"That was different." I crossed my arms, wishing he'd get to the point. The seconds were ticking down, and he hadn't come close to getting me to change my mind.

"Really?" He tilted his head, curious. "How so?"

"It doesn't matter." I didn't want to get into this again. "Why do you want to come with us so badly, anyway? Don't you have more important things you need to be doing?"

"More important than making sure you're safe?" He tilted his head, looking at me like the question was absurd. "Never."

It was something he would have said to me when we were dating, and the flash of the Thomas I knew from back then made my heart pang. But I forced the feeling away. Because while he might love me in his own way, he didn't want to *be* with me. And wasn't that what mattered?

Once this demon hunt was done, I'd go back to LA and Thomas would stay right here. Having him join us on this final hunt would just make it hurt more when this was all over.

"Look." I swallowed away a lump in my throat, needing

to get my feelings out there no matter how hard it would be. "I wouldn't have come here if it wasn't the only way to save Raven's life. You made your choice not to be with me, and I've accepted that. But these mind games you're trying to play with me… they need to stop. Just let me go. Please."

"I wish I could," he said. "But I can't. And I'm done trying."

He rushed toward me and lowered his lips to mine before I could say a word.

I realized what he was going to do a second before he did it, and my first instinct was to push him away. He couldn't break up with me and then kiss me and expect… well I don't know what he expected.

But once his lips were on mine, every rational thought disappeared from my mind. Fireworks exploded in my chest and warmth rushed through my body. I felt happier and more alive than ever. For years I'd been numb, guarded, and detached. It was like my soul had been broken, but now it was mending itself to become whole. More than whole.

It felt like it was joining with his.

I leaned into him, kissing him back with every bit of raw, passionate energy that had built up in me these past four years. From the way he kissed me back, it was like he felt exactly the same.

No... I *knew* he felt the same. I don't know how I knew. I just did.

Just as strongly as I could hear our hearts beating as one.

I broke the kiss and took a few steps back, staring up at him in shock.

"Sage." He spoke my name with so much desire that it took every ounce of my strength not to rush into his arms and kiss him again. "That was..." He ran his hand through his hair and shook his head, like he was searching for a word and couldn't find it.

I knew why.

Because what had just happened between us wasn't something that any vampire had ever experienced before. It wasn't something that *I'd* ever experienced before.

"It was different than any other time we kissed?" I guessed.

"You could say that." He looked at me in a daze, moved closer to me, and wrapped his arms around my waist. "What just happened between us?"

"It shouldn't be possible." I gazed up at him with wide eyes, feeling just as dumbfounded as he was. "But I think we just imprinted on each other."

30

RAVEN

I HAD no idea what had happened between Sage and Thomas in the dining room, but they both walked out of there looking like their worlds had been turned upside down. I wanted to get the dirty details—Sage was a friend, and something had *clearly* just gone down between them—but now wasn't the right time.

She mumbled that Thomas was going to come with us, and we got him up to speed on the technique we'd devised to reel the demons in and kill them before they had a chance to launch an attack.

The entire time we spoke, Thomas and Sage moved closer toward each other until their hands were nearly touching.

It was only when my hand brushed against Noah's that I realized we were doing the exact same thing.

"Fascinating," Thomas said once we'd finished explaining, although he focused on me. "So the demons are always drawn to you, and you have no idea why?"

"Yep," I said. "We're hoping to figure out why they're drawn to me once we get to Avalon. For now, we're just using it to help us on the hunt."

"Smart," he said.

"Thanks." I smiled, since it had been my idea. "I thought so too."

"So modest," Noah joked, throwing his arm around my shoulders and pulling me close to his chest.

I laughed and leaned into him, feeling more relaxed than ever. Which was crazy, since we were about to head out to hunt a demon. I should have been nervous or scared. But being with Noah—working with him like this—felt so *right*. No matter what happened, we'd get through it together and we'd be stronger for it. I knew it deep in my soul.

I still had so much ahead of me—getting to Avalon, passing the Angel Trials, and saving my mom. But as long as I was with Noah, I trusted that everything was going to work out.

Better than fine. Because I could no longer imagine my life without him in it. And despite his talk about how he didn't think we should mate because he wanted to protect me from never finding love again if he didn't make it through this war, I didn't think he could resist the connection between us any more than I could.

Time would tell, of course. But I had a good feeling about the two of us.

"All right, lovebirds." Sage snapped her fingers, bringing us back into focus. "Now that we're four instead of three, what's the best way to work Thomas into our plan?"

"It's been working best with the girls baiting the demons," Noah said to Thomas. "They pretend they've been drinking. With Sage wearing her cloaking ring, the demons assume Sage and Raven are two drunk human girls. The demons get cocky, making it ridiculously easy to lure them into the alley."

"It's easy unless the demon has backup," Thomas said. "Like the last one with the red-eyed shifter."

"Which is where you'll come into play," Noah said. "You'll stay back with me. We'll make sure no demonic supernaturals are following the demon and the girls. If we spot any, we'll take them down before they can follow them into the alley."

"Let's say we do find a red-eyed shifter," Thomas supposed. "While we're fighting it, what happens to the girls with the demon in the alley?"

"I can hold my own in a fight." Sage raised her chin

stubbornly. "At least, long enough until Noah can swoop in with the slicer and turn the demon to ashes."

"And what about you?" Thomas looked at me.

"The demon won't come into the alley without me," I said. "I might not be supernatural, but I'm the key to this whole plan working. Plus, Noah's been teaching me some self defense moves."

"I hope you don't have to use them," Thomas said. "Because if a demon attacks you, you don't stand a chance. Humans can be broken like twigs by super-naturals."

"It's a good thing the demons want me alive, then, isn't it?" I held his gaze, wanting him to know I wouldn't back down so easily.

He gave me a small smile of approval. "The Earth Angel is lucky to have someone as brave as you coming to Avalon to join her army," he said.

My cheeks heated, humbled by the compliment. At first, I'd only wanted to go to Avalon to save my mom. And of course I still wanted to save her—I *planned* on saving her. But as I'd been traveling with Noah and Sage, this fight had slowly become my own.

I couldn't wait to do my part in ridding the demons from the Earth once and for all.

"Raven's going to kick serious ass in the Angel Trials," Noah said, giving my hand a reassuring squeeze.

My stomach turned at the reminder that my journey had still barely begun. But I remained smiling, trying to stay strong.

"She'll make a powerful Nephilim," Thomas said. "But right now she's still human. And I'm not liking the idea of leaving the girls on their own tonight."

"They're not on their own," Noah said. "We'll be watching their backs, protecting them."

"I understand that," he said. "But what if we switch it up this time? You partner with Raven to lure the demon, and Sage and I will keep watch."

"The plan works best with two girls as bait," Sage said, scowling. "Don't you trust that I can hold my own until you and Noah arrive?"

"I know you can." Thomas gazed down at her, love and worry shining in his eyes. "But I just got you back. I don't want to let you out of my sight so soon."

Her expression softened—Thomas had clearly gotten to her. "I'll never be out of your sight," she said with a small smile. "You'll be following behind, able to see me the entire time. You'll be making sure Raven and I stay safe."

I looked back and forth between the two of them, more positive than ever from the adoring ways they were staring at each other that something big had just happened between them.

Resolve passed over Thomas's eyes, and he looked over at Noah. "You never let the girls out of your sight?" he asked.

"Never." Noah straightened. "I protect them with my life."

"As I will as well," Thomas said.

"I know you will," Noah said. "Welcome to the team." He held out his hand, and Thomas shook it with a single pump.

"Thanks for having me on it." Thomas glanced at each of us, and I could tell from the energy buzzing between the four of us that we were ready to roll. "So, what are we waiting around here for?" he asked, mischief creeping into his tone. "Don't we have a demon to hunt?"

31

RAVEN

BEFORE TURNING the corner onto the main street, Sage stopped at the end of the alley and uncapped the flask she was carrying in her jacket. She took a sip, swished the vodka in her mouth, and spit it out on the sidewalk. She handed it to me, and I did the same.

We couldn't afford to be drunk on the job, but we needed to convince the demons we were drinking. Swishing and spitting did the trick. That way we smelled like alcohol, but didn't have to deal with the dizzying effects of it.

The outside of the club had a line all the way out the door. But lines apparently didn't apply to Thomas. He simply walked up to the bouncer, looked him in the eyes, and said, "The four of us are on the list. Let us in."

The bouncer's face went slack and he unhooked the

rope, allowing us to walk inside without question. A few people in line—who I assumed had been waiting for quite some time—whined and complained. But we ignored them and walked on by.

It was definitely useful having a vampire prince on the team.

Inside was loud, bright, and so crowded that there was barely space to walk—just like every other bar or club we'd tracked the demons down in so far. It was a massive club, with multiple floors looking down from balconies to the center.

"There are five bars in here." Thomas stared blankly ahead, not focused on anything in particular. "The one in the back is the most crowded. Our friend is there." He blinked and refocused on Sage once he was done speaking.

Earlier, we'd filled him in on our lingo—how we called the demon our "friend" so we didn't sound suspicious.

"How do you know that?" I asked. Supernatural vision was better than human vision, but it didn't allow them to see through walls.

Or did it? It was probably safe not to assume anything anymore.

"I linked into the security cameras." He tapped his

forehead. "I can see every inch of this place right in here."

Technopath. Right.

Thomas was *definitely* coming in handy.

"Let's go." Sage linked her arm with mine, and we headed to the back bar. As a supernatural, Sage could see the demon's true form, so she always took the lead at this part.

I could only see a demon's true form when I knew to look for it. Even then, it only came in flashes. So I allowed Sage to pull me through the crowd. Unsure when the demon would spot us, I added in a few stumbles here and there.

It was important to keep up the facade of a drunk college girl from the start.

Sage pushed our way through the rows of people crowding around the bar. With her supernatural strength, she could have gotten to the front of all these humans with no problem. But she stopped midway through, peered over the sea of people, and let out a frustrated huff.

An attractive, well-dressed man in his mid-twenties was instantly by our side. The demon. It figured—the demons always took similar forms. Being attractive and appearing well off probably made it easier for them to lure in their prey.

"Do you ladies need help getting a drink from the bar?" He focused on me as he spoke. "On me, of course."

"Water." I giggled and stumbled into Sage.

She leaned into me and giggled as well, the two of us making a show of propping each other up. "I think we might have pre-gamed a *bit* too hard before coming out tonight." She laughed again and covered her mouth, as if she'd just revealed something she shouldn't have.

"Pre-gamed?" He glanced back and forth between us, looking truly confused. "What do you mean by that?"

Right—the demons had been locked in Hell for centuries. They understood English—during our drives, Sage and Noah had told me that both angels and demons were able to speak any language in the world.

But understanding English didn't make them versed in recent slang.

"We drank before coming out," Sage drawled. "A *lot*." She punctuated that with another stumble into me.

I pretended to lose my footing and fall straight into the demon.

"Ah." He caught my arm to steady me and eyed me up, smirking. "That explains your current inebriated state."

I swallowed down a shudder at his touch, forcing myself to smile instead.

I *hated* when the demons touched me. But practice was making me good at this.

"I can't believe you don't know what pre-gaming means!" I giggled again and tilted my head, like he entranced me. His eyes flashed red, and despite the urge to recoil, I pretended everything was normal. "You must not be from here," I continued without waiting for a reply. "Where are you from?"

"You're right that I'm not from here." He smirked. "I'm from down south."

"Ohhh." I raised my eyebrows, as if intrigued. "Like, Florida?"

"Nice," Sage said. "My grandparents live in Boca."

I couldn't help laughing—her grandparents totally didn't live in Boca. Actually, I didn't know much about her family besides Flint. If her parents or grandparents were still alive, she hadn't mentioned them.

The demon nodded, clearly having no idea where Boca was. "Are you girls from here?" he asked us.

"I have family out here and have been staying with them each summer for years," Sage said, swinging an arm around my neck and pulling me close. "Rebekah's my bestie, and she's staying with us for the week."

That was my code name for this hunt. Hers was Samantha.

"Rebekah." The demon eyed me up like a piece of meat. "A beautiful name for a beautiful woman."

Ugh. So cringe-worthy.

But I smiled anyway, since we had an act to keep up. "What's your name?" I asked, leaning forward in interest.

"Alex," he said.

Of course it was. The demons used code names too, and they picked the most common ones possible.

"Nice to meet you Alex," I said. Then I wrapped my arms around my stomach and groaned. "All that vodka's hitting me harder than I expected." I looked at Sage, pouting as if in pain. "I need food."

"Me too," she agreed. "Pizza?"

The demon's eyes lit up. "I'm getting hungry myself," he said. "Mind if I join?"

"Really?" I widened my eyes, as if thrilled he was offering to grace us with his presence. "I mean, I'd think someone like you would want to stay out, but if you want to join, that would be awesome!"

"Someone like me?" He studied me, suspicion sneaking into his tone.

My stomach dropped—had I just given away that I knew what he truly was?

I needed to cover, fast.

"I mean, someone as attractive as you." I lowered my

eyes, as if embarrassed for admitting it. Then I raised them slowly to meet his. "I thought you'd want to stay here partying."

"No need to stay out after meeting you." He smiled—predatory, again. "I found a great pizza place the other day—it's only a few blocks away. I hear it has the best pizza in Chicago. Want to check it out?"

"I've been coming here every summer since I was twelve," Sage cut in. "And despite my appearance, I have a voracious appetite. I *know* the best pizza place in all of Chicago. You can trust me on that."

"Maybe we're talking about the same place," he said.

"I doubt it." She flipped her hair over her shoulder and smiled. "It's a hidden gem—only locals know about it."

"She's right," I added. "It's *amazing*."

"Fine, fine." The demon held his hands up in defeat. "You win. Let's see if this pizza is as good as you claim."

That was quicker than expected—usually they put up more of a fight for us to go where they wanted. It was easier to get us to their designated alley that way.

At this point in the conversation, I typically had to pretend to get a text from a "twin sister" of mine saying she was going to meet us at the place we'd told the demon we were going. Since there was something about me the demons wanted, they never turned down the possibility of two for the price of one.

This demon was off his game. Maybe he'd indulged in one too many bourbons at the bar.

Bad for him—easier for us.

Sage and I led him out of the club, one of us hanging onto each of his arms. Judging by the sleazy grin on his face, he felt like the pimp of the century.

I couldn't *wait* to see his reaction when Noah followed us into the alley and rammed the slicer through his heart.

As we made our way out, a wave of warmth passed through my soul. Unsurprisingly, I caught a glimpse of Noah and Thomas standing near the exit.

At least now I understood why my soul felt like it was singing whenever Noah was nearby. It was because of the imprint bond.

Once out of the club, we led the way to the alley we'd chosen ahead of time. We continued with the charade of being drunk, and the demon was more than happy to keep his arms linked with ours to help us walk straight.

Thanks to the warmth of the imprint bond, I didn't have to turn around to know that Noah and Thomas were trailing behind. I also knew they hadn't encountered any of the red-eyed shifters. Good.

The hunt tonight had been easy so far. We were

getting better at this. Or maybe the universe was rewarding us for a job well done.

I couldn't wait for Noah to finish this demon off so we could get to Avalon and I could learn how to kick demon ass like the best of them.

As Sage turned the three of us onto a less crowded street, we were so close to ending this that I could practically taste it.

"Where exactly is this place?" the demon asked, glancing around at the thinning crowd.

"Just a little bit further," she said flirtatiously, stopping at the alley we'd selected. "Through here."

The demon stared into the alley, his eyes blank. "You girls are good." He smirked at Sage, and then turned his menacing gaze to me. He smiled, and I saw a flash of his pointed yellow teeth—what he truly looked like under the glamour. "Too bad I'm better."

Before I could ask what he meant, the buildings swirled around us, my stomach dropped down to my feet, and everything went dark.

NOAH

ONE SECOND THE girls were outside the alley, their arms linked through the demon's.

The next, all three of them were gone.

"Raven!" I screamed, slicer in hand as I ran to where they'd been standing. Icy dread coursed through my body. I felt around me, hoping they'd used invisibility potion or something, but the space was empty.

They were gone.

The warmth I felt from being near Raven was missing. The imprint bond was still there, but my chest felt hollow with a void I hadn't felt since leaving my pack behind in the Vale.

How could they be gone? I'd seen them. They were *right there.* This couldn't be possible…

I ran down the alley, hoping to find them there. Thomas followed at my heels.

Two red-eyed wolf shifters waited at the dead end.

I muttered a curse, shoved my slicer back into my weapons belt, and started to shift. Slicers were only useful on demons, and while these creatures *did* have the same red eyes as demons, Sage hadn't needed a slicer to kill whatever these creatures were. And we were better fighters in our animal forms.

Thomas was already expertly fighting the one on the left, and the one on the right jumped straight at me. I jumped as well, finishing shifting mid-air and sinking my teeth into his neck.

All of my anger from Raven's disappearance channeled through me, and I ripped the creature's head off with a ferocity I'd never fought with before. Blood splattered against the wall, and I dropped his body to the ground.

Whatever greater demon had taken Raven and Sage —and he *had* to be a greater demon, since he'd teleported away with them—had clearly been ready for us. He'd sent these demonic shifters to finish me off once he was gone.

Clearly he hadn't anticipated Thomas hunting with us, or he would have sent more than two of them. He'd also underestimated me, since I could have handled two of them on my own, but that was beside the point. Because with Thomas on my side, the demonic shifters didn't stand a chance.

I shifted back into human form just as Thomas was getting ready to finish his demonic shifter off.

But instead of going in for the final kill, Thomas held the shifter to the ground.

The wolf struggled against his hold, lying in a puddle of his own blood.

"What are you waiting for?" I growled and marched toward him. "Kill it so we can get out of here and figure out which greater demon just took our girls."

"We need to figure out what these shifters are and who they're working for," Thomas said calmly, not breaking his gaze from the red-eyed beast's. "We can't do that if they're both dead."

As badly as I wanted to shift back into wolf form and tear my teeth through the demonic shifter's throat, Thomas *did* have a point.

So I walked up to inspect the shifter, slicer in hand. The creature took deep, rattling breaths, his fur matted with blood. But despite how bad the wounds looked, he was already starting to heal. The blood loss would weaken him, but it wouldn't be long until he was ready to fight again.

We couldn't have that.

So I raised the slicer and jammed it through the wolf's shoulder.

The wolf howled in pain, going limp as I pulled the slicer out of the wound.

"What was that?" Thomas glared at me before turning his attention back to the demonic shifter still under his grip.

"An experiment." I twirled the slicer around in my hands, studying the shifter as he opened his red eyes again. "You see, this isn't any average blade. It was dipped in heavenly water by an angel, giving it the power to kill demons." I was saying this for the shifter's benefit, since Thomas knew all of this already. "You have the eyes of a demon, so I figured it would be fun to see what the blade would do to you."

The shifter bared his teeth and growled.

Thomas made a similar sound deep in his throat. "That was stupid and impulsive," he said, his grip on the shifter tightening. "What if it killed him?"

"I didn't stab him anywhere fatal," I said. "Yet."

Thomas pressed his lips together and kept his eyes on the shifter. He was difficult to read, so I wasn't sure if he was pleased or pissed. I was just glad he was on my side.

Like me, he'd do anything to get the girls back to safety. *Anything.*

"Take a look at that." I kept my eyes on the wound I'd inflicted, amusement creeping into my tone. "It isn't healing."

"You're right." Thomas now sounded equally as intrigued. "Try it again. This time, take off a finger. Better yet, a whole hand."

I stepped up, ready to do what was necessary to convince this creature to talk. Torture wasn't my thing —I liked to give my enemies quick, clean kills—but extreme times called for extreme measures.

If I had to torture this beast to find Raven and Sage, then so be it.

As I was raising the slicer in preparation to slice off his paw, the creature shifted back into human form.

He was a thin, scrawny thing who didn't look any older than sixteen. He must have been the runt of the litter. I would have thought he was harmless if it hadn't been for his creepy red eyes.

And for the fact that he'd just tried to kill us and was clearly working for the greater demon who'd taken Raven and Sage.

"Please," he begged, his lips trembling as he stared up at Thomas. "Don't."

"Tell us what you are, and who took the girls," Thomas commanded.

"I'm a shifter," he said. "And I don't know what girls you're talking about."

"Liar." I sneered down at him, and then looked to Thomas. "Can't you use compulsion on him?"

"I did," Thomas said. "He must be wearing wormwood."

I frisked the shifter's body as Thomas continued to hold him down. There were no wormwood pendants anywhere.

"Nothing," I said, turning to Thomas again. "Have you ever met a shifter immune to compulsion?"

"No," he said. "The only creatures immune to my compulsion are royal vampires, angels, and demons. So what are you?" He dug a finger in the wound I'd made with the slicer, and the boy winced in pain. "Because you're clearly not just a shifter."

"What gave it away?" The boy laughed. "Is it the eyes?"

I lunged at him, holding the slicer at his neck.

"Don't test me," I said. "Those girls who were just taken mean *everything* to me. Answer our questions, and you'll live. If not…" I paused, pressing the edge of the knife hard enough against his neck to draw a few droplets of blood. "You'll *wish* you were dead."

"Fine." The boy glared at me with dark hatred in his eyes. He'd transformed completely, no longer the trembling boy from a minute earlier. "You're right—I'm not *just* a shifter. I bound myself to a greater demon, which made me stronger than ever."

"How?" I rotated the angle of the slicer, pressing the tip of it into his neck. "Why?"

"As if I'll ever tell you," he said with a chilling smile. "By the way—Azazel sends his regards."

He pushed himself forward into my knife, still smiling as he gurgled up his blood and collapsed dead on the pavement.

I pulled my knife out of his neck and stared down at him in horror.

Our only lead was dead.

Raven and Sage were gone.

How had this happened? I'd never imagined tonight would end like this. From the horror and despair in Thomas's eyes, he hadn't, either.

But I wasn't going to back down so easily. Because while Sage and Raven were gone, they weren't dead. At least, Raven wasn't. If she were, I would have felt it through the imprint bond.

She was still alive—and I was going to make sure she stayed that way.

"Let's go." I looked away from the corpse and shoved the slicer back into my weapons belt.

"Where?" Thomas sounded like he was in shock.

"Back to the Bettencourt," I said, already making my way out of the alley. "And Cassandra better be there. Because she needs to do a tracking spell to find our girls."

33

RAVEN

ONE MOMENT I was looking into the alley, getting ready to help kick demon ass.

The next moment, I was in some kind of underground bunker—one of those places doomsdayers built to prepare for the end of the world. We were in a hall with lots of doors. It was dimly lit and old, rust all over the metal.

Whoever owned this place clearly stopped upkeeping it a long time ago.

Instantly going into self-defense mode, I let my arm go limp and pulled it out of the demon's hold. Sage had already reached for her dart full of potion that would force the demon—who was clearly a greater demon, since he'd teleported with us—back to his previous location.

The demon must have been prepared, because he swatted it out of her hand before she could jab him with it. It landed on the floor and he crushed it under his shoe.

Her eyes widened in panic.

But the demon was still focused on Sage. So I reached for my boot knife and surprise attacked him, shoving it straight into his back.

He didn't react at all—not even a flinch. I might as well have stabbed an inanimate object. He simply reached for the handle and pulled the knife out of his back.

"What'd you do that for?" he asked with the grin, tossing the knife down at my feet. "Messed up a perfectly nice jacket."

I knew regular knives couldn't kill demons—only slicers could do that—but this didn't look like it *hurt* him. It hadn't even drawn blood.

We were so totally screwed.

Sage growled and started shifting into wolf form.

I picked up my knife and bolted down the hall, hoping to find safety. I hated running, especially since I was leaving Sage to fight off the demon. But we'd trained for this. She was a supernatural and I wasn't. Getting out of this place and finding help was the most useful thing I could do to make sure we both survived.

I didn't make it far before the hall hit a dead end. Crap. I ran to each of the doors, trying to open them, but they were all locked. No amount of kicking or hitting them made them budge.

We were trapped.

I looked back over at Sage to see how she was faring against the demon just as three big men burst into the hall behind them. Flashes of red eyes and yellow teeth over their otherwise normal features showed me they were demons as well.

"Watch out!" I yelled to Sage, but it didn't matter. One of the demons had already thrown a potion pod of sludgy brown liquid at her. It was the same potion the demon in Nashville had used on Noah—the one that had stopped him from shifting.

Sage shifted back into human form, straining against the change the entire time. From the looks of it, the potion didn't just stop a shifter from shifting their animal form—it also forced a shifter already in their animal form to shift back to their human form.

Once human again, Sage breathed heavily on the ground, glaring up at the greater demon in hatred.

I ran up to help her, but one of the other demons grabbed me into a hold. I tried every self-defense move I'd learned to get out of it, but it was useless. I wasn't strong enough to fight supernaturals. Not as a human.

Sage got up and reached for her two boot knives, holding one in each hand and gearing up to fight.

The greater demon stepped back, motioning for his two other minions to take the lead.

Sage got a few good slices in, but in minutes, the two demon henchmen had disarmed her and were holding her steady between them.

The greater demon stepped toward her and removed a needle full of deep blue potion.

Complacent potion. How had he gotten a hold of that? Witches didn't sell complacent potion—they weren't even supposed to brew it. Using it was against the law because it took away free will.

Then again, these were demons. They wanted to erase all the supernaturals from the Earth. They clearly didn't care about following the law.

Stuck in the demon's grasp, I couldn't do anything but watch as the greater demon stepped up to Sage and injected her with the dark blue potion.

The fire disappeared from Sage's eyes, and she stopped fighting the demons' holds. Her expression slackened until she looked like a shell of her former self.

All I could do was watch in horror.

I hated being human. I was weak—a liability.

If I made it out of here and got to Avalon, I was

going to pass the Angel Trials no matter how hard they were.

I'd get turned into a Nephilim or die trying.

"That's better." The greater demon smiled at Sage. Then he turned to check on me. "Marco," he said, addressing the demon holding onto me. "Bring Raven over here. I want to see both girls' expressions during my big reveal."

Marco dragged me over until I stood next to Sage. She watched me hopelessly, a single tear slipping out of her eye and down her cheek.

We'd faced speed bumps on our hunts, but I'd always trusted we'd get through them and win.

Now, I wasn't so sure.

I tried to reach out to Noah through the imprint bond for help. The bond wasn't broken—something in me instinctively knew Noah was alive. But I couldn't *feel* him. His warmth was gone.

How far did the imprint connection reach? Was it possible that we were too far away for me to communicate with Noah?

"Where are we?" I asked the greater demon, on the off chance he might actually answer. "Why did you bring us here?"

"We're someplace where no one's going to find you," he said with an evil grin. His yellowed pointed teeth flashed over the illusion of his perfect ones, and I recoiled in disgust. "As for why I brought you here, you'll find out soon enough. But first," he said, turning to one of the demons holding onto Sage. "Give me the antidote pill."

"Be a good girl and stay right where you are," the demon cooed in her ear. "No more fighting, you hear?"

She nodded, her eyes panicked as he let go of her. It was like she wanted to fight, but she couldn't.

Stupid complacent potion.

The demon reached into his pocket, pulled out a pastel pink pill, and handed it to the greater demon. It looked like a Pepto-Bismol chewable tablet, and I knew from experience that it tasted similar to one, too.

The greater demon popped it into his mouth, chewed, and swallowed. The air around him went fuzzy and he morphed into someone I'd seen twice before—someone I would never, ever forget.

Azazel.

34

RAVEN

AZAZEL WORE the same leather jacket he'd had on the other times I saw him, and he grinned, clearly pleased with his dramatic revelation.

"Transformation potion." He flexed his hands, as if adjusting to being back in his body, and studied Sage and me. "From the looks on your faces, this wasn't how you expected your night to go, was it?"

Icy terror raced through my veins. This was it. Azazel was going to kill us, and there was nothing I could do to stop him.

Sorry, Mom, I thought, looking up to the ceiling and thinking of her. *I tried my hardest to save you. I'm so, so sorry I failed.*

The lapis lazuli charm necklace I was wearing—the one she'd given me for my twenty-first birthday—was warm against my skin. In that moment, it was almost like she was there with me.

If the Beyond truly existed, at least I'd be able to see her—and everyone else—again eventually.

"What are you waiting for?" I glared up at Azazel, trying to get somewhat of a grip on myself. "Why not just kill us and get it over with?"

I wasn't ready to die. But if I *had* to die now, I hoped it was quick and painless—if there was such a thing as a painless death.

"You think that's why you're here?" He laughed, so evil and chilling that the hairs on my arms stood on end. "You think I went through all that trouble of transforming my appearance, luring you into that trap in Chicago, and bringing you here... so I could kill you?"

"Why are we here then?" Sage asked.

"Don't speak." Azazel raised his hand to shut her up. "That question was rhetorical. If I wanted to kill you, you would have been dead a long time ago."

Sage pressed her lips together. Thanks to the complacent potion, she was unable to speak even if she wanted to.

At least they hadn't dosed me with complacent potion too. They must have thought I was weak enough as a human that they didn't need a drug to control me.

But as long as Azazel was talking, I wanted answers.

The more I knew, the better chance I stood at surviving this and saving my mom.

If my mom was still alive.

The possibility that she might not be crushed my soul. But back at the Pier, Rosella had said my mom was still alive.

I prayed she was right.

"So you don't want to kill us." I was relieved, even though it was too early to feel that way.

Honestly, I was just glad I wasn't about to die.

"I have other plans for your lovely shifter friend here." Azazel leered at Sage, and horror filled my stomach about what those other plans could be. "This isn't the final stop on Sage Montgomery's journey. However, I can't say the same for you, dear Raven."

I swallowed, fear taking hold again.

He *was* going to kill me.

I needed to get out of here.

Unfortunately, a human and a drugged shifter didn't stand a chance against three demons and a greater demon.

"Honestly, I'm not sure what I'm going to do with you yet," he continued. "My decision will depend on how willing you are to cooperate."

I glared at him, positive I'd never hated anyone as much as I hated him.

Because did I want to cooperate with Azazel? Hell no.

But I also wanted to live. The longer I stayed alive, the higher the chance that I'd eventually get out of here.

If that meant playing by Azazel's rules for now, then so be it.

I straightened and met his gaze straight on, determined to do anything necessary to survive this. "Cooperate with what?" I somehow managed to keep my voice cool and steady despite the rage flowing through my veins.

"Despite being human, I take it you're intelligent enough to have realized you're being hunted," he said.

I clenched my fists, furious at his assertion that humans lacked intelligence. "Yes," I said, forcing myself to control my rage. "I've noticed."

"And surely you've wondered what it is about you specifically that we want?" he asked.

"I have."

"I figured." He smiled again, clearly enjoying this.

"Are you going to tell me *why* you hunted me—and my mom?" I asked. "Or are you just telling me all this to toy with me?"

"It's certainly amusing toying with you," he said. "But you'll find out soon, so you might as well hear it from me."

I stared at him, waiting for him to spit it out.

When he did, it was the last thing I ever expected.

"We're hunting you because you're gifted," he said. "Because you have a unique ability that runs through your blood."

"Seriously?" I couldn't help it—I laughed. "I'm like, the least gifted person ever. My mom was the gifted one. Not me."

"Wrong," he said. "You're *both* gifted."

"How do you even know?" I humored him, since he sounded pretty confident that he was correct.

"The more gifted a human is, the brighter and stronger their aura," he said, as if it were simple science. "Most humans aren't gifted—their auras are watery and dull. Yours, my dear, shines like a beacon. As does your mom's."

"She's alive?" My heart leaped at the confirmation. Yes, I trusted Rosella, but it was different hearing Azazel speak about her in present tense. It made me more hopeful than ever.

"She is." He nodded. "Cooperate, and maybe you'll see her again."

I wanted to ask what would happen if I didn't cooperate, but I held my tongue. I already knew Azazel wouldn't hesitate to kill me. I couldn't bear him threatening my mom's life, too.

"How do I know you're telling the truth?" I asked instead.

"You don't." He looked to his demon guards, the conversation clearly over. "Lock her in with the others," he said as he walked over to Sage, wrapping his hand around her wrist. "I have business to attend to. It's time I reunite this docile little wolf with her pack."

I wished I could shake Sage into focus. But I couldn't escape the demon's hold, and shaking her wouldn't get that potion out of her system, anyway.

Instead, I stood there and watched as one of the demons walked to the door behind me and pressed his thumb against a little black square on the handle. A fingerprint reader.

The door swung open, revealing a room with about twenty people inside. The room reminded me of the hostels I "remembered" staying in when I thought I'd been backpacking around Europe—pretty bare minus the bunks lining the walls. The people inside were of various ages, and as far as I could tell, they all looked human. They wore matching blue jumpsuits, and looked fit and well fed.

None of them tried running out of the door to escape. The despair and hopelessness in their eyes showed they were just as thrilled to be there as I was.

"Meet your new bunkmates," the demon holding onto me said. "We'll be back with your uniform soon."

He shoved me inside, and I had one final glimpse of Azazel teleporting away with Sage before the heavy metal door slammed shut in my face.

35

FLINT

I WAS sound asleep when I was suddenly assaulted by the smoky smell of demon in my bedroom.

I jolted awake instantly. As the pack alpha, I'd trained myself to sleep lightly. It was my responsibility to be able to be awake and functioning at any moment in case of a threat.

I sat up, prepared to shift and fight. But I relaxed when I saw Azazel standing in the center of my room—with Sage by his side.

I smiled upon seeing my sister.

Then I noticed that Azazel's fingers were wrapped around her wrist, and she stared ahead emptily.

She looked traumatized.

What had Azazel done to her? She was supposed to

have arrived with Thomas, or with one of the other vampires from the Bettencourt coven. I'd expected her to come kicking and screaming.

I certainly hadn't expected this... emptiness.

My sister was usually warm, vibrant, and fiery. But looking at her now, I saw only a shell of who she normally was. If that.

Her body was there, but it was like her soul was gone.

"Sage." I said her name calmly, not wanting to alert her or Azazel to my alarm. "I'm so glad to see you." I rarely touched anyone—I was a guy who appreciated my personal space—but I walked forward and enveloped Sage in a hug.

She tensed, not returning my embrace.

I dropped my arms to my sides and took a step back. "What caused you to come to your senses?" I asked, looking back and forth from her to Azazel.

I really wanted to ask what he'd done to her, but I knew better than to anger him. We were so close to forming an alliance and ensuring the survival of the Montgomery pack. I couldn't mess that up now.

"Complacent potion." Azazel grinned, stroking Sage's arm. "You were right when you said your sister is strong and determined. It's a good thing I knew, so I could be prepared."

Sage's eyes looked pained at his touch, but she stayed where she was.

I hated seeing her like this. "I see." I nodded, focused on Sage. "Are you able to speak?"

"She was causing a commotion, so I told her not to," Azazel answered for her. "Thanks to the potion, she's abiding by my command."

"Well, she's here now, and she's not going anywhere," I said. "Surely you can give her the antidote?"

"Once the binding ceremony is complete, the complacent potion will no longer be necessary," he said. "But first, my witch needs to create a perimeter spell around your complex. I'll be back with her in a flash. Once the perimeter is made, I'll let you know so you can gather your pack in the backyard. Then, the ceremony can begin."

He teleported out, leaving me alone with my sister.

The moment he was gone, she removed her cloaking ring from her finger and dropped it onto the floor.

I'd rarely seen complacent potion in action, since it had been illegal since the Great War. But I knew how it worked. The person under its effect would do whatever they were told to do by the person standing closest to them.

With Azazel gone, I was that person.

"Put your cloaking ring back on," I commanded. I

had no idea who she thought was going to come for her —Noah was supposed to be dead by now—but it wasn't worth the risk. "And *keep* it on."

She glared at me as she leaned down to pick up the ring and slid it back on her finger. She shook the entire time, like she was fighting against the potion. But while my sister was strong, the potion Azazel had given her was stronger.

It forced her to obey me, but she still looked at me like she hated me.

I felt better knowing she wouldn't hate me for long. Now that I could properly explain what was going on, I'd get her to come to her senses.

I'd been readying myself for this conversation for days.

"You can speak," I said, bracing myself for the onslaught I knew was coming.

She stared up at me in horror—like she didn't know me anymore. "What have you done?" she asked, the four words making far more of an impact than the full-blown rant I'd expected.

"I did what I needed to do to keep you alive." I crossed my arms, standing my ground. "To keep our *pack* alive."

"You're working with Azazel." She spoke slowly—timidly. Like she wanted me to deny it.

I couldn't.

I hated the disappointed way she was looking at me. But when the Montgomery pack survived this war and came out on top, she'd be grateful. They all would be.

She didn't see it now. But she would then.

"Why?" she asked.

I supposed she took my silence for what it was— admittance that I was doing what she accused.

"Hundreds of demons have been released onto the Earth, and they're more powerful than shifters, vampires, and witches combined," I said. "They can't be injured by our weapons. Our teeth and claws do nothing to them. They want to rule the Earth, and they plan on exterminating all supernaturals that stand against them. We can't beat them. Our only option is to join them."

"That's not true." Sage raised her chin defiantly. "Heavenly weapons can kill them. I've seen it myself."

"Noah is the *only* supernatural in possession of a heavenly weapon," I said. "For all we know, it's the only one of its kind. One blade cannot defeat an army of hundreds, no matter how skilled its wielder."

"There are more," she insisted. "The Earth Angel is at Avalon now. She's training an army as we speak."

"The Earth Angel hasn't been heard from in months!" I clenched my fists, wanting to shake some sense into my innocent, idealistic sister. "If she's leading this so-called army, where is it? Why aren't they doing anything to help?"

"They're not ready yet," she said. "They're waiting—"

"For what?" I interrupted. "No one who has gone to Avalon has ever returned. We can't even be sure that Avalon *exists*. For all we know, it's a plot created by the demons. Lure the rebels to a mysterious island with an unknown location and kill them before they become a bigger threat than they already are."

"It's not," Sage said. "The Earth Angel exists. Avalon exists."

"You've been there?" I raised an eyebrow, already knowing her answer.

"No." She bit her lip, although she held her gaze with mine. "But it exists. I *know* it does." Her eyes shined with so much conviction that I knew she believed it down to her core.

She was so sweet and naive. I needed to protect her now more than ever.

"Your blind faith is humbling, sister." I placed my hands on her shoulders, hoping to get through to her. "But in times of war, faith won't keep you alive. You know what will? Alliances. Family. *Pack*." I looked at her, willing her to understand. "I need you to trust me—as your brother, and as your alpha—to make the alliances necessary to keep our pack alive. Can you do that? For me? Please?"

36

FLINT

FOR A MOMENT, I thought I'd gotten through to her.

I was wrong.

"I'm not the one with blind faith." Sage stepped back and scowled, as if she couldn't bear to have me touch her. "You are. You're the one who's trusting a *demon*—a creature you admitted yourself wants to kill our kind— to stay loyal to a so-called alliance."

"I know it must seem crazy to you," I said. "I get that. But you don't know the whole story."

"Then tell me." She tilted her head and narrowed her eyes, clearly doubting me. "What's the whole story?"

"Azazel has a daughter," I said. "Her name is Mara."

"Demons can have children?" She sounded beyond skeptical.

"They can," I confirmed. "As can angels. It's harder

for immortals to reproduce than creatures on Earth, and their pregnancies last much longer than ours. But yes, they can have children."

"Azazel told you this?" she asked.

"Mara did," I said. "After we imprinted on each other."

"You *what?*" Sage's eyes widened, her horror growing. She looked like she couldn't believe what I was telling her.

I couldn't blame her. Before it had happened, I would have had a similar reaction myself. "I know it sounds impossible," I said. "And I don't have an explanation for how it happened. But when I first saw Mara, I was drawn to her. Then, when we kissed, I imprinted her. And she imprinted back." I watched my sister, waiting for her to say something—anything. Waiting for her to say she didn't believe me.

She didn't. She was still looking at me in horror, but she didn't deny my claim.

"You believe me?" This part was going better than I'd expected.

"The rules are apparently changing," she said. "Noah and Raven imprinted on each other, too. And I..." She paused and ran her fingers through her tangled hair, looking more conflicted than ever.

"You what?" I probed.

"Nothing." The indecision in her eyes disappeared. "I just don't understand why you and Noah were able to imprint on other supernatural races. It shouldn't be possible."

"It certainly has never happened before," I said. "But it's happening now."

"I understand this must be... confusing for you," she said cautiously. "But just because you imprinted on one demon doesn't mean you can trust all of them. It doesn't even mean you can trust *her*. Maybe the demons are behind us suddenly being able to imprint on other races. Have you ever thought about that?"

"Mara was just as surprised by our connection as I was," I said.

"Or she was pretending to be." Sage rolled her eyes.

I took a few deep breaths, fighting off the urge to protect Mara's integrity. Once Sage met Mara, she'd understand.

Until then, she needed to know about the rest of the deal I'd made with Azazel.

"The alliance with Azazel is thanks to Mara—thanks to our imprinting on each other," I said calmly. "She went to him and asked him to work with us. Once our pack binds ourselves to Azazel, he's given Mara and I permission to mate. We'll join their family. Azazel will protect us like we're his own."

Sage nodded, resolution entering her eyes.

For the first time since she'd arrived, I started to breathe easier. She was finally starting to see things clearly.

"You're really going to go through with this, aren't you?" she asked, her voice small.

"I am." I nodded. "*We* are. This alliance will be legendary. It will save our pack. You're my sister, and I might not say it enough, but I love you, Sage. I've always promised that I'll do anything to protect us, and I have. A war worse than anything the Earth has ever seen is coming. Thanks to this alliance, we're going to survive it. And we're going to come out stronger for it."

"I understand," she said slowly, although she looked like she was about to break down where she stood.

"Good." I smiled and reached for her, so she could take my hand. "I knew you'd come around."

"No." She stared at my hand, not taking it. "I understand that you believe you're doing the right thing. But the right thing for you isn't the right thing for me. If you truly love me like you say you do, then let me go. Please."

"Go?" I lowered my hand, anger rushing through my veins. "Where?"

"I'll take one of the cars and drive to Amber's," she said, sounding desperate now. "She and the others in her circle will get me to Avalon. You might not believe

Avalon exists, but I *know* it does. I'll be safe there. Away from all of this."

"No." I shook my head, unable to believe this. "Even if I wanted to allow it, I couldn't. Azazel would know I'd let you go. It would ruin everything I've built for us."

"Azazel's a *demon!*" Hatred flared in her eyes. "Imprinting on Mara has blinded you, but it hasn't blinded me. Once Azazel's gotten all the use from you that he needs, he'll destroy you. He'll destroy us all." Her voice was dark—haunted. She believed what she was saying with every ounce of her soul.

I backed away, realization setting in. Sage was brainwashed by Noah's fantasies of the Earth Angel saving the world from a magical island that probably didn't exist. An island that no one who had gone to had ever returned from.

The truth was that the angels weren't going to help us. If they were going to, they would have come already. Instead, they were hiding out in Heaven, doing nothing. The angels didn't care about us. They never would.

But Sage wasn't going to understand any of that. At least not until the binding ceremony with Azazel was complete.

I was starting to see why Azazel had commanded her not to speak. I'd always admired my sister for speaking her mind no matter what, but it was too painful seeing her refuse to face reality.

"Azazel will return soon with Mara and their witch," I said, keeping all emotion from my tone. "Sit down while we wait for him. And no more speaking. I see now that there's no getting through to you, and I can't listen to this idealistic nonsense any longer."

She did as I said, shaking and glaring at me the entire time.

I tried to hold on to the hope that once the blood binding ceremony was over, she'd forgive me.

But from the way she was looking at me—like I was the enemy instead of her brother who loved her and was doing everything to protect her—I was starting to wonder if she ever truly would.

37

FLINT

AZAZEL TELEPORTED BACK to my bedroom an hour later. This time, he was accompanied by Mara and a dark haired witch.

Mara hurried to my side the moment they arrived. "It's time," she said with a knowing smile. She glanced at Sage and asked, "Is this your sister?"

I also glanced at Sage, who was still sitting in the armchair I'd commanded her to. Her arms were crossed, and while she couldn't speak, her eyes fumed with revulsion. "Yes," I said. Wanting to show a united front, I reached for Mara's hand and took it in mine. "This is Sage. Azazel found her and brought her back home so she can take part in the ceremony."

"Welcome, Sage." Mara smiled warmly. "I hope you

find as good of a fortune with one of my brothers as I've found with yours."

Sage's eyes widened, and she shook her head in horror. Her eyes begged me to release her.

But of course, I wouldn't.

Mara turned to me, confused. "You didn't tell her?" she asked.

"I told her about you and me," I assured her. "As for the rest... I thought it best to wait until after the binding ceremony is complete."

"I understand." She lowered her eyes. "I'm sure she's still mourning the loss of the shifter she imprinted on and ran off with."

That was the cover story I'd told them, since I doubted Azazel would have taken too kindly to knowing Sage was on a hunt with the First Prophet to kill demons.

"As discussed, her boyfriend has been taken care of," Azazel said simply.

Shifters never referred to the people we imprinted on as boyfriends or girlfriends, but I dared not correct Azazel.

Sage's expression collapsed in devastation, a few tears running down her face.

I looked away from her, unable to see her in such pain.

The only relief I had was that once the blood binding ceremony was complete, her pain would feel like it was from a lifetime ago.

"Wonderful," I said, although I said a silent prayer that Noah would have an easy transition to the Beyond. "I have faith she'll be as lucky as Mara and I have been."

"She better be." Azazel twisted a piece of Sage's hair around his finger and smiled down at her. "How come you never told me she has such an... agreeable appearance?"

I swallowed, not liking where this was going. "She's my sister," I replied, remaining as neutral as possible. If Azazel suspected that the thought of his being attracted to Sage disgusted me, we'd have a problem on our hands. "I don't look at her that way."

"Of course, of course." Azazel released the strand of her hair, although he remained close to her. "Anyway, I've been quite rude, as I still haven't introduced you to Lavinia here." He motioned to the witch he'd brought with him, and I turned my focus to her.

With her pale skin and jet-black hair, she looked like a ghost. Especially given the long white nightgown she wore that touched the floor. Apparently I wasn't the only one of us here who'd been woken from a slumber. And like all dark witches, her magic smelled sickly sweet, like syrup that had been sitting out for too long and was starting to coagulate.

"Lavinia comes from a long line of dark witches," Azazel continued. "Like you, she also recognizes a great opportunity for an alliance when it presents itself."

"Pleasure." I nodded at her.

"Likewise." She didn't move as she spoke.

Azazel watched the exchange with pride—like a pet owner when two of their animals took a liking to one another. "While you were in here watching your sister, Lavinia cast a perimeter spell around the complex," he said. "Until the blood binding spell is complete, no one will be able to leave the property."

"That's some very powerful dark magic," I said.

"I'm a very powerful witch," Lavinia replied.

Mara stepped closer to me, apparently not liking the way Lavinia was looking at me. I couldn't blame her— Lavinia looked like she wanted to eat me alive. However, I suspected the witch looked at everyone that way. It was just the nature of her features.

The humans had a name for that look.

Oh, right. Resting bitch face.

Azazel looked at each of us and smiled, apparently pleased by the outcome of this meeting. His gaze lingered on Sage's for extra long before returning to mine. "Now that the perimeter spell is up and we're all introduced, it's time for you to wake your pack," he said. "Because we have a blood binding ceremony to complete."

FLINT

As PLANNED, Azazel, Mara, and Lavinia waited in my room with Sage as I woke the pack and brought them outside. My pack mates weren't thrilled to be woken up in the dead of night, but since it was a command from their alpha, they grumbled and dealt with it.

It didn't take long to gather them in the yard. The moon wasn't out, making it a darker night than most, and I looked around to double check that everyone was there. They were.

The Montgomery pack was large—there were twenty-six of us in all, which was why we needed such a large complex to house all of us. An average pack had between six to ten members. Anything larger than that usually resulted in more than one alpha. When that happened, the pack would split.

The Montgomery pack was the strongest in the country, so even the most dominant of our members submitted to me. No one wanted to leave a pack as powerful as ours. Large packs had drama, yes, but I never failed to keep them in line.

"I'm sure you're wondering why I've woken you in the middle of the night," I said, and a chorus of nods showed me that yes, they were.

I stepped atop a large slab of rock, ready to say what I'd rehearsed many times leading up to this moment.

"As you know, dark times are ahead." I looked around at all of them, my tone grave and serious. "Hundreds of demons have been released from Hell—creatures with powers greater than any supernatural on Earth can comprehend. As shifters, we're strong, but our powers are no match to the demons. It won't be long until the demons take their place on the top of the food chain and eliminate all supernaturals that try to defy them. Our time as the apex predator has sadly reached its end."

Unhappy grumbling sounded from the crowd, concern flashing in the eyes of my pack mates.

I held out my hands to silence them, and they watched me expectantly. "I know this isn't what you expected to hear," I said. "The truth isn't always easy to swallow. However, as your alpha, I take my duty to protect each and every one of you seriously—your lives are as precious to me as my own. For weeks, I've been searching for a way to ensure our safety. And tonight, I'm pleased to tell you that I've found the solution—an alliance that guarantees the Montgomery pack will remain alive and protected in the times to come."

I paused to scan their eyes, pleased to find them watching me breathlessly, waiting for me to continue.

"Actually, it's fairer to say that this alliance found me." I chuckled, pretending that this part was unrehearsed. "Last week, when I imprinted on the woman who will soon become my mate."

On cue, Azazel teleported in with Mara.

She stood beside me, flanked on the other side by Azazel. Lavinia had also teleported in with Sage, although the two of them stood off to the side, so they wouldn't steal my thunder.

Gasps erupted from the crowd, and my two strongest men shifted and rushed at Azazel.

"Stop!" I commanded, but I was too late.

In seconds, Azazel reached for his sword and beheaded them, leaving their corpses bleeding out at our feet.

The moment they died, their bonds to the pack broke and chills rushed to my bones.

I glanced down at their bodies in horror. I hadn't given Azazel permission to kill members of my pack.

He was supposed to want them alive. The men who were dead at our feet were future numbers who would have been on our side.

"Why did you do that?" I asked Azazel, shocked.

"They tried to attack me," he said simply. "You saw."

"They didn't have a chance to understand what I'd done for them—what *you* were offering them." I clenched my fists, furious at him for killing *my* pack mates—and *his* future alliance—so callously. "They didn't know what they were doing. Once they knew, they would have apologized. They would have been on our side."

If my plea affected the greater demon at all, I couldn't tell. He just stared at me emptily, and then looked out at the members of my pack.

Most of them gazed up at him in horror. Two women held onto each other in tears—the mates of the men who had died.

The men Azazel had *murdered*.

"Let them serve as an example." Azazel stepped up and pointed at the bodies at his feet, his voice echoing throughout the yard. "You will listen to what your alpha has to say," he commanded. "Flint has made an alliance that will keep you alive. You have no idea how lucky you are to be part of the Montgomery pack. But if you don't hear him out—if you react like these two did—you're not going to remain alive for long enough to hear about this incredible opportunity you're being offered. Understood?"

Seeing Azazel destroy two of our strongest warriors so easily must have scared the rest of my pack into submission, because they remained silent.

"Fantastic." Azazel smiled and looked to me. "Flint, please continue."

I continued on to tell them all about Mara. She stood strong next to me the entire time, despite numerous pack members looking at her in disgust and disdain. As I told the story, the disgust lessened on some of their faces, but not all.

I hated seeing them look at her like that. I wanted them to see her beauty as much as I did.

They would. Once the blood binding ceremony was complete, they would.

"I'm the first shifter to imprint outside of our species," I finished, looking out at them in pride. "This is *not* a coincidence. It's a sign. A sign that I—Flint, the alpha of the Montgomery pack, the strongest pack in the country —is meant to make this alliance. You saw Azazel's power just now!" I glanced down at the two dead men at my feet, my stomach churning at how their deaths were coming in handy. But I didn't let it show. Because I'd do anything to show my pack the truth, even if that meant using the death of our two strongest men to help them understand. "Once the blood binding ceremony is complete, we'll protect Azazel, and we'll be under his protection. We'll be invincible! After the war, we won't just survive—we'll thrive!" I raised my fist into the air at the end, punctuating the finale of my speech and looking into the eyes of each of my pack mates to get my message across.

By now, a few of them were smiling and nodding. But when I reached Sage, she was watching me like I was a total stranger.

I clenched my fist tighter, refusing to let her get to me. Under the complacent potion, she *would* go through with this. She was going to get Azazel's protection whether she wanted it or not.

But we didn't have complacent potion for anyone else. So I looked away from my sister and refocused on the rest of my pack, determined to get all of them to understand. Determined to *save* them.

I refused to have any more casualties like the two men at my feet.

"I've brought this opportunity straight to our doorstep." I lowered my voice, more serious now than ever. "I did this for you—for our pack. I'm your alpha, and this alliance with Azazel is my choice. More than that—it's *fate's* choice, by having me imprint on Mara. So now, I ask—will you follow me? Will you complete the blood binding ceremony with me today to commit to Azazel and make our pack stronger than it's ever been before?"

Most of them chorused yes. Even the ones who looked scared.

Three of them who were standing to the side of the pack—a husband, a woman, and their child—shifted and made a run for it.

They didn't get far before colliding with an invisible barrier. The perimeter spell.

The woman—Joanie—shifted back into human form and banged her fists against the barrier. "No!" she screamed. "Let us out! We won't tell anyone what you're doing. Just please—let us go."

Her husband Kevin and son Michael shifted into human form while she was talking. Kevin placed a hand lovingly on her shoulder, and she wrapped an arm protectively around her child.

She looked to me, as if I was still the one in charge here.

I wished I could tell them that Azazel would give them another chance.

But I knew the greater demon better than that. I also knew their fate wasn't in my hands. Not anymore.

Azazel teleported over to them in an instant. Before I could blink, he ripped Kevin's head off his shoulders and dropped it to the ground like a bowling ball.

Joanie fell to her knees and wailed. She was one of the most submissive wolves in the pack. She wouldn't try to fight.

"You're just going to stand by and watch him do this to us?" She looked at our pack mates standing before me and pointed to Azazel. "We're your pack. We deserve better than this... monster." She looked up at Azazel when she said the final word, her eyes blazing with hatred.

Azazel shoved his hand into her chest and yanked out her still-beating heart.

Her eyes went blank and she collapsed to the ground. No one said a word as they watched her fall. The silence weighed down heavy upon us, like a blanket.

A blanket of fear.

Next, the greater demon turned to Michael.

The boy trembled, looking down at what remained of his parents in shock.

I knew what he was going through. The tragedy was so recent that it still hadn't had time to settle in... it didn't feel real to him yet. There was no saying what he'd do now.

I held my breath, preparing for the worst.

Azazel let go of Joanie's bloody heart, letting it fall to the ground next to Michael's feet. "Did you truly want to flee and reject this great opportunity I'm giving you?" he asked, backing the boy against the edge of the boundary. "Or were you just following your parents and doing what they said?"

Michael looked to me in fear. The boy was only eight years old. With his parents gone, he was looking to me— his alpha—for guidance.

I gave him a single nod, hoping he understood what he needed to do to survive.

Michael swallowed and looked back up at the great demon towering before him. "I... was following my parents." His voice shook, and he stared up at Azazel in terror. "I'm sorry."

Azazel said nothing. He just studied the boy, as if he was waiting for something else.

Everyone was silent. I could barely breathe as I waited for what Azazel was going to do next.

"Your Grace," Azazel corrected him. "You'll call me Your Grace."

Michael lowered his eyes, blinking away tears. "Your Grace," he repeated. "I'm sorry, Your Grace."

After what felt like the longest few seconds of my life, Azazel grinned. "Fantastic." He reached for Michael's hand and led him—well, more like dragged him—back to the rest of the pack. Once they reached us, he held up their joined hands in victory and said, "It's time for the blood binding ceremony to begin!"

39

SAGE

I STOOD by Lavinia's side the entire time my brother addressed our pack, trapped in my own body by the complacent potion. I couldn't speak. I couldn't move.

All I could do was watch in horror.

Azazel led Michael back to the pack, and the young boy's eyes were empty in shock and terror.

At the sight of him, all of my hope that this might somehow stop was sucked out of me. Flint had somehow convinced the pack to buy into his crazy belief that we were *meant* to enter into this alliance with a demon. And for those who hadn't drank the "team up with demons Kool-Aid," Azazel had literally terrified them into submission.

The beginning of the end of the world was happening, and I was just standing there watching it.

With so much going on, no one paid me any attention. Thanks to my silence, my pack mates must have assumed I supported Flint's decision.

Stupid complacent potion.

Time was running out. Under this potion, Flint could command me to take part in the blood binding spell. I didn't know what a blood binding spell with a demon was like, but it couldn't be good.

The last thing I wanted was to be bound to Azazel.

What would happen to me if I were forced to go through with it?

I didn't know, and I didn't want to find out. But I couldn't fight. I couldn't speak. Even if I could, what could I do? Azazel was powerful beyond belief. If I spoke out against him, he'd kill me. If I ran, I'd crash into the perimeter spell. And then he'd kill me.

The only way out of this was death.

I needed help. If only I could just get the cloaking ring off my finger. Then maybe someone—hopefully Thomas or Noah—would be able to locate me and do something.

I tried to push past the complacent potion and reach for the ring. But just like every time before, nothing happened.

I needed to fight harder. So, staring at Azazel, I let all my hatred for him bubble to the surface. His red eyes shined with evil as he surveyed the pack, his hand still holding onto the boy's.

This monster was taking *everything* from me. My brother, my pack, my freedom—they were all going to be gone. And it was all because of Azazel.

I couldn't let that happen. Especially because I'd just gotten what I'd craved for so long—I'd imprinted. And not just on anyone. I'd imprinted on Thomas. The man who'd owned my heart for so many years.

My future with him was being snatched away from me before I'd gotten a chance to taste it.

If only the imprint bond worked across far distances. Then I could reach out to Thomas, tell him where I was, and he could do something to help.

Unfortunately, communication through an imprint bond only worked when you could see the other person. Anything further required a full out mate bond.

Thomas could only find me if he could track me. And I refused to let the kiss we'd had a few hours ago be our last.

With that thought, my hand started to move toward my cloaking ring. Slowly, as to not catch Lavinia's attention, but it moved. Soon, I was sliding the ring off my finger, forcing my expression to remain neutral as I dropped it to the ground next to my feet.

I glanced at Lavinia to see if she'd noticed. She

hadn't. She was completely focused on Azazel. Apparently she was so convinced that I'd be unable to fight the complacent potion that she was barely paying me any attention.

Freedom burst forth from my chest.

With the cloaking ring removed, Thomas would be able to find me.

Fighting against the potion had taken all my energy, but I'd done what I could. Hope wasn't lost.

"Lavinia." Azazel looked at the witch and smiled in anticipation. "Bring forth the goblet. Sage, come stand next to your brother. It's time for us to form a circle so the blood binding ceremony can begin."

40

SAGE

OF COURSE, I did as Azazel instructed and walked to stand beside Flint. The complacent potion gave me no other choice.

Even if I *could* still fight against the potion—which I couldn't, since every bit of my energy had been used to take that ring off—I didn't want to die. Now that I'd imprinted on Thomas, I had too much to live for. Especially now that he'd be able to track me.

Lavinia walked behind a nearby tree and pulled out a large pewter goblet and a matching dagger. She must have stowed it there when she'd cast the perimeter spell and prepared the grounds for the ceremony.

The dark witch approached Azazel, holding the goblet and dagger out before him. "Your Grace." She stared up at him, her eyes gleaming with anticipation. "We start with your blood."

Azazel took the dagger and carved a vertical gash along his forearm. Such a cut would have mortally wounded a human—but he didn't even grimace. He just held his arm above the goblet and allowed his blood to seep from his body and flow into the chalice.

"Enough," Lavinia said once he'd given so much blood that the goblet must have been halfway full.

Azazel pulled his arm away, the gash knitting itself together. In seconds, the wound was healed.

Lavinia took the dagger. Holding both it and the goblet, she turned to Flint, who was standing proudly by Azazel's side. "I won't need as much blood from you and the members of your pack," she said. "Only a drop. Use the dagger and take the blood from your palm."

Flint did as instructed, allowing a drop of his blood to fall into the goblet. Then he handed the dagger to me.

I stared at the weapon in my hand, dread filling my soul.

"Go on, Sage," Lavinia purred, stroking the goblet. "It's just one drop."

I glanced around the circle. For the first time tonight, everyone's eyes were on me.

Not one of those pairs of eyes shined with hope. They were either scared or resolved.

I never would have believed that the Montgomery pack could have been beaten into such submission if I wasn't here to witness it myself.

If Azazel could do this to us, what were the demons going to do to the supernaturals all over the world?

It hurt my heart to think about it. If the Earth Angel and her army didn't start doing something soon... we were doomed.

"Sage." Flint seethed. "Cut your palm with the dagger and add a drop of your blood to the goblet. Now."

The complacent potion took hold of the command, and my body started acting on its own. I pricked my palm with the dagger, held it over the goblet, and allowed a drop of my blood to fall into the chalice.

I choked down a cry, understanding why complacent potions were illegal. No one should be allowed to control another person like this. Ever.

"Perfect." Lavinia took the dagger from me and continued around the circle, collecting drops of blood from each member of the Montgomery pack. The only person who didn't participate in the ceremony was Mara. Once Lavinia made her way back to Azazel, she brought the chalice into the center of the circle and added her own blood to the mix.

Then she reached into the inside pocket of her jacket and pulled out a vial. "Lastly, the blood of someone I've recently killed," she said with a chilling smile, uncapping the vial and dumping its contents into the chalice.

When the vial was empty, she tossed it to the ground and used both hands to hold the goblet in front of her. She stared into it and started chanting in Latin.

The wind whipped around us, and a silver glow surrounded the goblet, growing larger and larger as she chanted. Eventually, the light radiated out to fill the entire circle, bathing us in its chilling glow. When I breathed in, coldness filled me to the bone. It was like I could *feel* the evil of the spell all the way down to my soul.

How did Flint still think this was the right decision? I glanced to the side to look at him, but he stared blankly ahead. Whatever he was thinking, I couldn't get a read on him.

Lavinia stopped chanting, and the silver light disappeared. It took my eyes a second to readjust to the moonless night.

"It's ready." She walked to Azazel and handed the goblet to him. "His Grace will drink first, and then he'll pass the chalice around the circle. This spell is strong and dark, so remember to only take a sip. Anything more will likely be lethal." Her tone was laced with warning as she spoke the final sentence.

Azazel took a sip from the goblet and passed it to

Flint, who then swallowed the blood and lowered the goblet, turning to me.

I gasped at the sight of his eyes. Because my brother's familiar brown eyes were gone. Now they were red. Demon red.

Just like the shifters who'd attacked me, Noah, and Raven in the alley in Nashville. Whoever those shifters were, they'd completed a blood binding ceremony with a demon. It had done something to them—something that had changed them deep within.

People sometimes said that eyes were the window to the soul.

Did this ceremony just change my brother's soul?

"Take the goblet," Flint commanded. "Drink."

I took the goblet from him, my hands shaking. The pewter material was cold, like it had just come out of a freezer. The blood inside smelled dirty and tainted.

I didn't want to drink it. But given the circumstances —including the complacent potion still running through my veins—I didn't have a choice.

I glanced over at my cloaking ring. It was still on the ground outside the circle, where I'd been standing before the ceremony.

Thank the angels I'd been able to fight past the complacent potion for long enough to remove the ring. Otherwise, all hope would have been lost.

Please Thomas, I thought as I raised the goblet to my lips. *Find me. Together, we'll fight this. Because no matter what this blood binding ceremony does to me, I love you, and I promise my heart will always be yours.*

Despite the chalice being cold, the blood was warm when it touched my tongue. It tasted bitter and sticky. I forced it down, pressing my lips together in disgust as I swallowed.

It was a good thing we didn't need to take any more than a sip. I didn't think I would have been able to endure it.

The blood settled into my stomach, the darkness seeping from my center all the way to the ends of my fingers and toes. I thought it would have felt cold, or uncomfortable. But it didn't.

It felt safe. Like a blanket giving me protection I hadn't realized I'd needed. I felt strong. Invincible. Calm.

Before, my emotions had been a swirling mess, like a hurricane. Now they were tranquil and steady. I saw everything clearly now.

It was all thanks to Azazel. And Flint, of course, for having the sense to make this alliance. I'd have to apologize to my brother later for giving him such a hard time about this. By making this alliance, Flint was keeping me safe. He was keeping the entire *pack* safe. I understood that now. I was grateful.

I turned to the shifter next to me—a woman named Marie who was a few years older than me. We'd never had much in common—she was a big gossip, so I'd never trusted her with anything meaningful—but she was always fun to hang out with.

She took a sharp breath inward when her eyes met mine.

"Don't worry," I assured her, handing the goblet to her. "You'll feel so much better after you drink."

Once she took the goblet from me, I walked out of the circle, toward where I'd been standing earlier.

"Where are you going?" Flint asked.

I leaned down and picked up my cloaking ring from the grass, examining it with a knowing smile. "I must have dropped this during the excitement earlier," I said, sliding the ring back onto my finger where it belonged. "It's a good thing I noticed. There are some people who might be looking for me—we wouldn't want them to find us and bring trouble to our pack."

"No." Flint smiled as I rejoined his side. "We most certainly wouldn't."

I watched as the goblet made its way around the circle. Once each shifter drank, their eyes turned red and they visibly relaxed. Finally, the goblet made its way to the final member of the Montgomery pack—Michael, who stood on Azazel's other side.

The young boy looked terrified as he raised the goblet to his lips.

But once he drank, his eyes turned red and he was calm like the rest of us.

"Wonderful," Azazel said as Lavinia took the empty goblet from Michael's hands. "Now that you're bound to me, you have my protection, as I have yours. We're an alliance. A *family*. And I'm pleased to officially give your alpha Flint Montgomery permission to mate with my daughter Mara."

Flint bowed his head to Azazel. "Thank you, Your Grace," he said.

"You're welcome," Azazel replied. "We'll have to celebrate, since the first mating between a demon and shifter will be a moment that will go down in history."

"Yes." Flint smiled at Mara, who beamed in return. "It certainly will."

"And I have to admit that it's gotten me curious," Azazel continued. "If a shifter can imprint on a demon, what about a greater demon? Could one of you imprint on me?" He tilted his head in curiosity, letting his gaze meet everyone's in the circle. Eventually he focused on me, his eyes lingering up and down my body for much longer than any of the others.

Whatever he was looking for, I hoped it pleased him.

"Sage Montgomery." My name sounded like honey as

he spoke it. "You're strong, smart, and beautiful. If I'm able to imprint on a shifter, I want it to be you."

I widened my eyes in surprise. "Thank you, Your Grace," I said, lowering my head to show him the proper respect. "You honor me greatly."

"I know." He smirked, appearing to enjoy this. Good. I wanted him to be happy. "And I don't want to wait to find out," he continued. "Come here now and kiss me."

I walked toward him, my eyes locked on his. He was so handsome—like a god.

But as I approached, I felt a stirring deep within. I wasn't sure what it was... but it seemed to be trying to tell me something.

It was telling me to stop. To remember something important—a feeling I was supposed to have. Not for Azazel, or for anyone in the pack.

It was a feeling for someone else. An important promise I'd made him.

A promise my heart was begging me not to break.

"Sage?" Azazel's voice snapped me out of my thoughts. "Is everything okay?"

I blinked, comforted by the caring way my master gazed down at me. The reminder of his protection made whatever I'd been feeling before disappear in an instant.

What *had* I been feeling before?

I wasn't sure, but I needed to answer Azazel's question. It was rude to keep him waiting.

"I'm just nervous, I suppose." I shrugged and smiled, feeling silly for causing my master to worry. "It's not every day that I'm selected for such an honor."

"Understandable." He twisted a strand of my hair around his finger and leaned closer, focused only on me. "How about you put an end to those nerves and kiss me now?"

"I'd love to." With that, I rested my hands against his chest, stood up on my tiptoes, and pressed my lips to his.

I hope you enjoyed The Angel Trap! If so, I'd love if you left a review. Reviews help readers find the book, and I read each and every one of them :)

Reviews for the first book in the series are the most helpful. Here's the link on Amazon where you can leave your review ➜ The Angel Trials

---

The next book in the series—The Angel Gift—is out now.

Get your copy now at:

mybook.to/angelgift

You can also take a look at the gorgeous cover below. (You might have to turn the page to see the cover.)

Everyone is separated, and no one is safe.

Raven Danvers didn't think her life could get any crazier since the night a demon attacked her in an alley and abducted her mom.

She was wrong.

Because now that same demon has abducted her too. He's thrown her into a secret bunker with a group of humans who have unique abilities that make them "gifted." They don't know what the demons want with them, and the bunker is impossible to escape.

Her only hope is Noah—the wolf shifter she's imprinted upon. She just needs to let him know where she is. But she can't do it alone. Her only way to get a message to him is to team up with the other humans by making use of their unique gifts.

But they have to do it fast. Because their time in the bunker is temporary. The demons are prepping them to go somewhere else... somewhere far worse than where they are now.

They don't know what this place is.

They just know they really, really don't want to find out.

Get ready for a magical, twist-filled ride in the fourth installment of The Angel Trials series, a fast-paced urban fantasy adventure that will leave you on the edge of your seat wanting more!

Get your copy now at:
mybook.to/angelgift

Also, make sure you never miss a new release by signing up to get emails and/or texts when my books come out!

Sign up for emails: michellemadow.com/subscribe

Sign up for texts: michellemadow.com/texts

And if you want to hang out with me and other readers of my books, make sure to join my Facebook group: www.facebook.com/groups/michellemadow

Thanks for reading my books, and I look forward to chatting with you!

ABOUT THE AUTHOR

Michelle Madow is a USA Today bestselling author of fast-paced fantasy novels that will leave you turning the pages wanting more! Her books are full of magic, adventure, romance, and twists you'll never see coming.

Michelle grew up in Maryland, and now lives in Florida. She's loved reading for as long as she can remember. She wrote her first book in her junior year of college and hasn't stopped writing since! She also loves traveling, and has been to all seven continents. Someday, she hopes to travel the world for a year on a cruise ship.

Visit author.to/MichelleMadow to view a full list of Michelle's novels on Amazon.

THE ANGEL TRAP

Published by Dreamscape Publishing

Copyright © 2018 Michelle Madow

ISBN: 1722489057
ISBN-13: 978-1722489052

❀ Created with Vellum

68546817R00163